BETRAYAL

Looks Far was never certain exactly what Blackbird intended. He may have been desperately trying to convince the enemy chief of their sincerity. On the other hand, his tortured spirit may have completely abandoned sanity. He may have intended to attack Lame Bear.

In any event, it made no difference. In the space of a heartbeat, one of the enemy warriors struck out with a stone war ax. Blackbird slumped into the dust. The other warriors pressed forward.

"We come in peace!" Looks Far shouted, simultaneously raising his hand in the peace sign once more.

He did not have time to look around to see what the rest of his party was doing. Something struck him across the back of the head and he felt himself sliding from the horse. His consciousness was fading, but his last thought was of failure. This had been the People's only chance for survival in their Sacred Hills.

Now with darkness rushing in, the chance was gone. . . .

Bantam books by Don Coldsmith
Ask your bookseller for the books you have missed.

The Sacred Hills

>> >> >> >> >> >> >> >> >> >>

DON   COLDSMITH

BANTAM BOOKS
TORONTO · NEW YORK · LONDON · SYDNEY · AUCKLAND

RL 6, IL age 12 and up

*This edition contains the complete text
of the original hardcover edition.*
NOT ONE WORD HAS BEEN OMITTED.

THE SACRED HILLS

*A Bantam Book / published by arrangement with
Doubleday, a division of Bantam Doubleday Dell
Publishing Group, Inc.*

PRINTING HISTORY
*Doubleday edition published August 1985
Bantam edition / October 1988*

ISBN 0-553-27460-0

Published simultaneously in the United States and Canada

*Bantam Books are published by Bantam Books, a division of
Bantam Doubleday Dell Publishing Group, Inc. Its trademark,
consisting of the words "Bantam Books" and the portrayal
of a rooster, is Registered in U.S. Patent and Trademark
Office and in other countries. Marca Registrada. Bantam
Books, 666 Fifth Avenue, New York, New York 10103.*

PRINTED IN THE UNITED STATES OF AMERICA

KR   0 9 8 7 6 5 4 3 2 1

Introduction
by James Hoy
» » »

The Sacred Hills is my favorite of the novels in Don Coldsmith's Spanish Bit Saga. This book, as with the other titles in this collection of historical fiction, appeals because of its clean plot line, its plausibility of character, and its accuracy of situation. The particular attraction of this book for me, however, is its setting, the Flint Hills of Kansas, an area of quiet beauty and special attribute rarely portrayed in literature.

One of Coldsmith's strengths as a writer is his ability to universalize. Readers have variously thought the People to be Kiowa or Cheyenne or Comanche or Osage or Plains Apache. As Coldsmith himself notes, however, his People are in reality a composite, a generic (to use this oft-maligned word in its original and positive sense) plains tribe that combines traits and traces from a number of tribes into a fictional People every bit as realistic as any who historically roamed the central plains.

In setting, as well, the author has created landscapes that allow each reader to see the meadows, mountains, valleys, and hills of his or her own area of the plains—or imagination. Some years back, for instance, a reviewer commented on the accuracy with which Coldsmith had portrayed a particular bit of countryside (Wyoming, as I recall) when the scene that was actually in the author's mind as he wrote was a hill in Chase County, a few dozen miles west of his Emporia, Kansas, home. Much of this same latitude for the exercise of the reader's geographic imagination is preserved in *The Sacred Hills*, yet at the same time Coldsmith has explicitly placed the People in the tallgrass range country of the Flint Hills, quietly evoking in an occasional descriptive detail the special quality of these Hills.

The Flint Hills of Kansas, forming a band approximately 50 miles wide, start near the Nebraska border (north of present-day Manhattan) and run south nearly 200 miles, at which point they merge into the Osage Hills of Oklahoma. This area, together with the row of counties bordering the Flint Hills to the east, is sometimes labelled the Bluestem Grazing Region, its 4,000,000 acres of native grass a small remnant of the tallgrass prairie that once stretched north to Canada and east to Ohio. At the time of the action in this novel, of course, this native grass was still undisturbed, except for those few acres cultivated by the Growers.

In time the Flint Hills stretch back nearly 300,000,000 years to the Permian Period of the Paleozoic Era. Over the eons as wind and water smoothed much of the center of the North American continent into the comparatively level grassland we call the Great Plains, layers of limestone permeated with bands of flint (or, more properly, chert) protected the ridges of what are now the Flint Hills, the sides eroding away to form valleys and canyons. While much of this region is distinctly hilly, it is not overly rough (in comparison, say, to the Gypsum Hills of Kansas, the Black Hills of South Dakota, or the Missouri River Badlands of North Dakota) nor are any of the hills particularly tall—perhaps 1500 feet above sea level. Still, lying as they do between rolling wooded land and small farms to the east and flat wheat land to the west, the emerald-grass Flint Hills stand out uniquely in modern-day Kansas.

Cutting through the Flint Hills are a number of rivers—among them the Kaw and the Blue in the north; the Cottonwood, the Neosho, and the Verdigris in the middle; and the Walnut and Fall Rivers in the south. These rivers, along with the numerous small streams and springs of the Hills, would have supplied a group of Native Americans such as the People with fish and ample water. Today many watershed dams and ponds dot the Flint Hills, but the springs still gush and the streams still run clear.

Another resource that might have drawn the People to the Flint Hills is wood. While the hilltops and slopes and valleys themselves are grass-covered with only an occasional tree, the banks of the streams and rivers are lined with forests of oak, elm, sycamore, ash, hickory, and hackberry. The trees around Council Grove were especially prized by Santa Fe traders as a source of hardwood for repair of wagons. Many of the trees in the Flint Hills today, the oaks and sycamores especially, are over a century-and-a-half old, predating white settlement.

Anglo-Americans began to settle the Flint Hills within a year or two after the opening of Kansas Territory in 1854, although the oldest town in the Hills, Council Grove, traces its origin back to 1825 when government officials met with representatives of the Osage tribe in order to secure peace along the recently opened Santa Fe Trail. The Osage had been roaming in the general region of the southern Flint Hills (and eastern Kansas, western Missouri) for some two centuries by this time, arriving at approximately the same time that the Kansa (or Kaw) Indians had moved into the northern part of Kansas and of the Hills. In their time of freedom both tribes maintained villages in western Missouri and eastern Kansas, making regular trips out onto the High Plains to hunt bison. Later both tribes (along with several others) were given reservations in eastern Kansas and, still later, northeastern Oklahoma. The Kansa actually occupied two different reservations in the heart of the Flint Hills near Council Grove, once fending off an attack by marauding Cheyenne while their white neighbors came out from the town to watch the battle from surrounding hilltops.

The Native American history of the Flint Hills goes

back much further than either the Osage or the Kansa, however. The popularity of this area as a pathway for north-south migrations and as a site for permanent villages and camps lends support to Coldsmith's assertion that different tribes might have considered the Hills a special, even a holy, place. Ceramic materials and other Woodland native artifacts from the Flint Hills, for instance, have been carbon dated to around 350 A.D., while Paleo-Indian artifacts dating back to 10,000 B.C. have been discovered throughout the region.

Archaeologists have also located and examined sites where Native Americans mined flint for the making of tools—scrapers, knives, spearheads, arrowheads. While much of the flint (or chert) in the Flint Hills is found within small pockets of limestone rocks, some of it also exists in layers, and where these layers cropped out to the surface Native Americans would gather to cut "blanks" to be taken back to their villages for more detailed work. Stone artifacts were (and are) plentiful at various sites throughout the Flint Hills, but especially so along the South Fork River in Chase County (a river, like the Verdigris, with bluffs steep enough to have served as a model for the bison-stampede ambush in *The Sacred Hills*). In the first half of this century Frank and George Roniger (bachelor brothers who farmed near the small cattle-shipping town of Bazaar in Chase County) collected stone tools so successfully that they amassed what was at the time the largest private collection of arrowheads in the nation. Much of their collection, by the way, is on display at the museum bearing their name in the county seat town of Cottonwood Falls.

Early in Chapter Four of this novel, Dr. Coldsmith touches on the practice of burning old grass in order to attract game to the new growth, a practice especially effective in a tallgrass region. This brief allusion is fraught with meaning for those who know the Flint Hills, for the Native American custom of firing the prairie was adopted here early on by white settlers whose descendants maintain the custom to the present day. At one time the deliberate, regular burning of pasture ground was undertaken virtually nationwide, but by the second quarter of this century the practice had fallen victim to popular and scientific opposition. Burning on a large scale continued only in the Flint Hills and there as a folk custom among farmers and ranchers who burned in open defiance of accepted wisdom. By the 1960s, however, that wisdom changed as range management specialists discovered through experimentation what the ranchers, and before them the Native Americans, knew from experience—that deliberate burning created better pasture for livestock, whether cattle, horses, or bison.

Native Americans throughout the Great Plains burned for many reasons—to signal, as a weapon in warfare, to drive game, or, through the growth of new grass, to attract game. Historical documentation of burning in the Flint Hills by both the Kansa and the Osage can be found in the accounts of early white travelers in the region, while folk tradition links to-day's burning by ranchers directly to that done by the native peoples. Flint Hills ranchers, for instance, tell of Native Americans weaving huge balls of long-stemmed bluestem grass, then attaching a rawhide lariat to the ball, setting it afire, and dragging it across the prairie from the back of a running horse.

The ensuing fires must have been extensive and spectacular, burning everything from river to river. A desirable side effect of such burning was to keep the tallgrass prairie free of trees, but the immediate result was to attract game, for new bluestem, the richest of prairie grasses, will spring up within days of an April burn. That the burning did indeed attract game into the Flint Hills is proven both by the accounts of early white explorers and settlers (who note in particular buffalo, deer, elk, and antelope) and by the many buffalo wallows still visible today in Flint Hills pastures. The buffalo, Coldsmith's narrator says, come and go, like the seasons, and undoubtedly the fall and winter months would have found the Flint Hills free of bison, for bluestem, while nutritious in the spring and summer, quickly loses its food value in the cold months, a time when the bison would migrate out onto the buffalo grass of the High Plains.

Although Coldsmith's main purpose is narrative not descriptive, he does include a short passage here and there that accurately portrays the beauty of the Flint Hills, that describes color or scenery or vegetation or wildlife, passages that help to explain why both the People and the Head Splitters consider the Hills a sacred place. A major reason for their importance to the two tribes is because of the resources—game, water, wood—that are to be found therein, but these mundane qualities do not explain fully the love for the tallgrass prairie that both Looks Far and Wolf's Head express.

Their feelings, and those of their fellow tribesmen, it seems to me, result not just from the productivity of the Hills but also from the physical beauty that mirrors a spiritual strength that comes from deep within them. In mythic terms, hills (or other high places) are almost invariably associated with the divine. Moses is called onto a mountain in order to receive the Law. Noah's world-saving voyage ended on a mountaintop. In *The Faerie Queene* the Red Crosse Knight attains purity and sees a vision of Truth while on a mountain. The Sioux, the Cheyenne, and the Crow all considered the Black Hills sacred; it was, in fact, to Harney Peak (highest point in the Black Hills) that Black Elk, holy man of the Ogalalla, was transported in his great vision.

For whatever reason, perhaps because we feel closer to the divine or perhaps because from a hill we can see farther and with greater clarity, human beings of all cultures seem spiritually drawn to high places. "I will lift up mine eyes unto the hills, from whence cometh my help," sang the psalmist: for Looks Far that statement was literally true. It was from a hilltop that the bison stampede both destroyed his enemies and provided winter food for his tribe. More important, it was the Sacred Hills that brought together, for the first time, two warring tribes; love for the land proved stronger than human animosities. The Flint Hills were indeed a holy place for the People.

—*Emporia State University*
  Emporia, Kansas
  January, 1988

Preface
» » »

$\mathbf{A}$mong the tribal religions of the Native American, there is a recurring theme, that of the Sacred Places. On the earth's surface are special locations, places where spiritual strength emerges from the land, affecting the lives of people under its influence.

It is possible for the Sacred Places to influence not only one, but also a series of cultures through the centuries. Mount Sinai, the temple sites of ancient Greece, the city of Jerusalem, and the special cathedral locations of Europe and Britain may be examples. The spiritual qualities of such sites do not exist *because* people have designated them so. The reverse is true. The Spirit was there before people came to these areas to recognize their importance.

On the North American continent, the most familiar of the Sacred Places may be Devil's Tower in Wyoming. Blue Lake in New Mexico is another such location, part of the religion of the Taos Pueblo. The "Garden of the Gods" in Colorado is not idly named. Who can stand in the awesome grandeur of such sites without feeling the Spirits of the places?

But not all Sacred Places are as magnificent and awe-inspiring. Each tribe has claimed its own Sacred Places, and there may be entire areas that are of spiritual significance. There may be major Sacred Places, perhaps surrounded by lesser sites, forming an entire region that provides spiritual sustenance to the people

1

who use it. It is perhaps significant that the Native American seldom assigns a personality or name to this spiritual entity. It is merely that Spirit which inhabits the Sacred Place.

To the People, buffalo hunters of the tallgrass prairie, their sustaining Spirits inhabit the Sacred Hills.

1

>> >> >>

The invaders came from the north, spreading across the prairie like the buffalo in their seasonal migration, or rather, like the hordes of grasshoppers which, in a season of evil medicine, sometimes devoured everything in their path.

Yes, the newcomers were like grasshoppers, destructive without apparent purpose. The buffalo came, furnished food, shelter and garments for the People, and moved on, leaving the prairie none the worse for their passing.

This strange, warlike tribe seemed to belie every common custom of the people of the plains. No one knew from where they had come, somewhere far away in the northern mountains. They observed none of the social amenities usually accepted even among traditional enemies. The Head Splitters, rivals of the People for the same hunting grounds, were at least predictable.

Actually, the Head Splitters had proved little trouble for a generation. Since the coming of the horse, the People had rapidly become a power to be reckoned with on the plains. After a few major battles, and especially after the era of the warrior woman, Running Eagle, conflict between these two traditional enemies had become a stable thing. There was a sort of armed truce, each tribe respecting the potential danger of the other.

True, there were occasional ambushes of small hunting parties, the constant horse-stealing raids, and the accidental confrontations during seasonal moves to new campsites. Children, especially young girls, might be stolen by the Head Splitters if occasion offered. The beauty of the women of the People was legendary. Still, there had been no major battles since Running Eagle's War.

It was not that the People had become soft. Their fighting strength was at its greatest, and the far-flung bands competed with each other at the annual Sun Dance and Big Council. Each band was proud of its herds of elk-dogs, some of the finest anywhere on the plains. Theirs was a complacency that comes from self-confidence in one's own strength. It was a strength that had not been required in war in recent seasons, but only in the hunt. Life was good for the People. The children were fat and the women happy, and there was enough meat for all.

That was until the coming of the Blue Paint People, dealing death and destruction. It seemed they were everywhere at once, along the northern margins of the territory used by the People.

Even the Growers, who could get along with anyone, were not immune to their depredation. It was the Growers, in fact, who had first warned of the terrorists from the north. These quiet people, in small farming villages along the streams, traded their products to any and all for meat, skins, or whatever was offered. Their neutral position was respected by all.

Until the coming of the Blue Paints. The strangers had ridden into an isolated Grower village, it was said, in the Moon of Falling Leaves. There was no warning whatever. They had begun to kill, burn, and loot. They had carried off the entire year's crops of corn, beans, and dried pumpkins, burned the half-underground lodges, and killed the inhabitants. The few survivors had managed to reach another Grower village, and it was in this way that the story had eventually reached the People.

Winter had prevented further activity by anyone.

There had been no further word of the invaders. Many of the People were of the opinion that there was no problem at all. Some distant village of Growers, far to the north, had been attacked by a tribe of their own area. It was of no concern to the People. If the attackers were invaders, then they must have returned to their own country by now.

There were those among the People, however, who suspected the worst. An enemy in great strength, in strange country, would need great amounts of food. One way to obtain it would be to plunder the supplies of unwary tribes like the Growers.

One whose thoughts ran along these lines was the medicine man, Horse Seeker. He was one of the few among the People who had had firsthand experience with the Blue Paints.

It had been many seasons ago, while on his medicine quest. He had traveled far to the mountains of the northwest, and had fought and defeated Walks-Like-Thunder, a fearful leader of the Blue Paints. His victory would never have been possible, he knew, without the medicine of the Dream Horse.

Ah, but that was long ago. Now his eyes were dim, though his mind and body were sound. Horse Seeker knew that when the rumors of the Blue Paints filtered to his, the Southern, or Elk-dog band, there was trouble ahead. He was certain that the despoilers of the Growers' village to the north had not returned to their own country.

Somewhere, in great strength, the Blue Paints lay in waiting in their winter camp, waiting for the coming of spring. Then they would strike.

Horse Seeker felt the anxious prickle of the hair on his neck, the wetness of his palms. He remembered the feeling of fear as if it were yesterday, in the far country of his wife's people.

"This is not good, Yellow Bird," he commented when she had finished relating the news.

A couple of young men from the Northern band had undertaken a winter trip to visit relatives and had brought the story. The attack on the Growers was now several moons ago.

It was only because of an uncommonly mild stretch of winter weather in the Moon of Hunger that the People were moving about a little. There had been scanty snow, and Horse Seeker realized that with the coming Moon of Awakening, the threat of the Blue Paints would increase.

He thought now of the danger to the Northern band of the People, the nearest to the advance of the invaders.

If, indeed, that was their purpose. Perhaps he was wrong, overly anxious because of his handicapped vision. But no, there was the possibility of real danger here.

"Yellow Bird," he spoke solemnly, "I would talk with Looks Far. He should warn his wife's people."

Their only son, Looks Far, had married well, to a girl from one of the best families in the Northern band. The couple had quickly produced two children, a boy and a girl.

Yes, he must talk to Looks Far.

2

"**Y**es, Father, you wished me to come?"

Looks Far straightened and blinked in the semidarkness of the lodge. His father sat across from the doorway, smoking his long-stemmed pipe. Fragrant blue smoke curled upward, intertwining with that from the fire in the center of the lodge.

Yellow Bird let the door-skin fall behind her, and moved quietly around the fire, beginning to prepare the evening meal.

"Come, my son, sit with me," Horse Seeker beckoned. "We must talk."

The younger man sank to the offered pile of robes, and waited for his father to begin. Horse Seeker smoked in silence for a time, then cleared his throat.

"Looks Far, you have heard of the raid by Blue Paints from the north?"

"Yes, Father, but that was against the Growers, not the People."

Horse Seeker nodded impatiently.

"I know, I know. But that does not matter. They are the enemies of all. I have seen them."

For a moment, Looks Far thought that his father referred to a mind-picture in his head. With his eyesight failing, Horse Seeker seemed sometimes to see that which others could not. But, no, Yellow Bird was nodding agreement. Then he remembered. His father must be referring to his experiences long ago, among Yellow Bird's people.

"It is true, my son. The Blue Paints are an evil tribe. Listen to your father."

"I have thought," Horse Seeker continued, "that your wife's people should be warned."

"But, Father, the Northern band is the strongest of the People!"

"Yes, I know. But, Looks Far, they do not know this enemy as I do. They must be warned. You must go and tell them."

"Tell them what, Father? They know the Growers were attacked. It was they who told us!"

"No, you must go to the Real-chief. Tell Yellow Hawk what I have said."

There was an urgency in the voice of the older medicine man. Well, thought Looks Far, it might be well to do so. It could do no harm. A pleasant journey, as spring awakened the prairie, would be a welcome change. His wife, Chickadee, would welcome a chance to see her parents.

"It is good," he nodded. "We will go tomorrow if the weather is good."

"But you must be careful, my son."

"Of course. There will be no danger this early in the season."

It was true. The weather would be too unpredictable for another moon, at least, for war parties to move freely.

Chickadee was elated. She moved rapidly around the lodge, assembling the odds and ends of supplies necessary for the journey. She welcomed the chance to escape from the boredom and restricted activity of the winter moons. The children, too, were excited. Seldom was there an opportunity to visit their grandparents.

Looks Far went to the lodge of Standing Bird, chief of the Elk-dog band. As a young man, he had been one of the first, it was said, to learn the medicine of the elk-dog. It was partly because of this, Looks Far knew, that Standing Bird had become chief after the death of Heads Off.

The young medicine man could barely remember his great-grandfather, the outsider whose memory was now revered as the bringer of the First Elk-dog. Looks Far remembered Heads Off as a quiet, fatherly man with snowy white fur upon his face. He had been very old.

Now, Standing Bird himself showed the snows of many winters in his hair. He had been a capable chief.

Looks Far approached the chief's lodge and tapped against the taut skin cover.

"My chief," he called, "it is Looks Far."

He was welcomed inside, where the old chief motioned him to sit.

"Uncle," he began, using the People's traditional term of respect for any adult male, "I would speak with you of a journey."

Standing Bird nodded, waiting.

"My father wishes me to take a warning to the Northern band."

"A warning?"

"Yes, he is alarmed at the news of the Blue Paints to the north."

Standing Bird nodded, somewhat puzzled.

"But their raid was against the Growers."

"My father fears that they mean more evil. He has fought the Blue Paints, you know."

"Yes, I remember. His was a great victory, it is said. But why does he think the Northern band needs warning?"

"I do not know, myself," Looks Far shrugged. "But they are closest to the danger. My father sees things, sometimes."

Standing Bird nodded agreeably.

"Yes, his medicine is strong. So, when do you go?"

"Tomorrow. I will take my family to visit Chickadee's people. Is there any message you wish me to give the Real-chief?"

"No, only tell him we will meet at the Sun Dance."

"Of course. We meet at Elk River?"

The chief nodded.

"It is good."

Looks Far rose to depart. It was only custom, the formality of tradition, that made him offer to carry a message to the Real-chief. Yet in a deeper sense it was one of the niceties of the People's culture. It was such things that made the young medicine man proud of his tribe. It was a reassuring thing, the polite byplay that implied respect and honor to both leaders.

He ducked through the doorway into the dusk of evening, and threaded among the lodges to his own. Chickadee was feeding the children, and paused to set out food for her husband, also.

"We will leave the lodge up," she mentioned conversationally. "We will return before the band moves."

Looks Far nodded, only half listening. He was choosing, in his mind, the horses they would take. In the interests of a light, fast journey, even the children would be mounted.

Both were proficient riders, though only three and five summers old. The children of the People could often ride before they could walk. It was not unusual to tie an infant on the back of a trusted old mare, to rock gently with the animal's motion as she grazed near the camp. The child would doze, or wake and watch the changing scenes of activity, secure in the close contact with the mother-warmth of the horse. It is little wonder that among the Elk-dog People, riding had become as natural as walking.

Sun Boy had barely thrust his torch above earth's rim when the family of Looks Far was ready to depart. Chickadee carefully adjusted the smoke poles, closing the flaps tightly against inclement weather. She tied the door-skin in place and turned to her horse.

The chill of the morning had not yet begun to lift as they stopped before the lodge of Horse Seeker and Yellow Bird.

"Hurry back," Yellow Bird admonished.

"Of course, Mother," Chickadee chuckled happily, looking forward to a visit with her own parents. "We will see you soon."

Horse Seeker watched them go through the mists of his failing vision. He could see only the shape and color of their movements as they turned to ride away. He could not have explained why he was concerned. There was only the vague, ill-defined feeling that all was not right, somehow.

The heart of Horse Seeker was very heavy.

3

» » »

The trip was pleasant. Ducks and geese flew overhead in long lines, traveling in the same direction as the little party. Swelling buds on the trees told of the Moon of Awakening. The prairie was not yet greening, but in sheltered areas along the watercourses, tiny shoots came to life in promise.

Along the marshy places, hordes of tiny spring frogs trilled a chorus of continual sound. A great blue heron stalked among them in the shallow water, eagerly hunting. The shrill frog-song ceased as the bird stepped near, rising again behind it.

Looks Far turned aside to catch and show the children one of the frogs. It was tiny, no bigger than his thumbnail. It blinked solemnly as it sat crouched, unmoving in his palm.

"This is Little-Frog-With-Loud-Voice," he told the children while they giggled, delighted. "He will be your friend. If danger approaches, he stops singing. Then you may look and see if it means danger to you, too."

He released the tiny gray-green thing, and it took one long leap to disappear in a puddle.

"We will see you again, Little Brother," Looks Far spoke gently.

They remounted and rode on.

For only one day the weather was too forbidding to travel. Wet flakes of snow spattered down during most of the day, and Sun Boy never appeared. The family of Looks Far took shelter in a thick patch of heavy timber to wait out the spring storm.

They saw no other travelers, though Looks Far was cautious as they moved. Many times he rode ahead to scan the country to the north for any sign of danger. But none was seen, and the journey proved uneventful.

The little party arrived at the Northern band's winter camp, and Chickadee took the children to find her parents' lodge. Looks Far made his way to pay his respects to the chief.

"*Ah-koh*, my son," Yellow Hawk greeted, apparently not surprised. "Come and sit."

"*Ah-koh*, uncle. I am Looks Far, of the Southern band. I come to visit my wife's people, and I bring greetings from Standing Bird."

The older man nodded. He had already learned the young man's identity before his arrival. His scouts were alert.

"Yes, of course. Your father is Horse Seeker."

"Yes. He is one of my reasons for coming."

The chief frowned, puzzled.

"What does he wish?"

"Nothing, my chief. He only wished to warn you."

He paused, embarrassed. It seemed illogical, somehow. He was here on a mission to warn the Real-chief who was also leader of the most powerful band of the People. How could this matter be stated?

"You know, my chief, that a village of Growers was destroyed before the winter moons, by invaders?"

The chief nodded, waiting.

"My father, Horse Seeker, wishes for me to tell you of these invaders. He has met them before."

"Ah, yes. He reached their country on his vision quest long ago, did he not?"

Looks Far nodded affirmatively.

"He would have come himself to warn you, but his sight is failing."

"That is unfortunate. But tell me. What of his warning?"

"Only this, my chief. Horse Seeker says to tell you

that these Blue Paints are evil. Their number is like
grains of sand, and they kill merely for pleasure. He
thinks that they mean to take our hunting grounds,
our Sacred Hills, from us."

The chief was silent a long time. He relighted his
pipe with a twig from the fire and blew a cloud upward toward the smoke hole. Looks Far waited.

"You do not believe this, Looks Far?"

"I do not know, my chief. I only brought the
message."

"But you have brought your family on this journey.
Surely you thought there was little danger."

Looks Far was impressed that the Real-chief had
already learned this much, almost before their arrival.
He was off-balance, embarrassed again. Truly, there
was reason for this thoughtful man to be Real-chief.

"Yes, my chief. I felt little danger this early. In
another moon, I would not do so."

The chief nodded, apparently satisfied.

"It is good, Looks Far. Now, I too have wondered
about these Blue Paints. They took all the Growers'
crops. They must be many. And I believe they will
come farther this way. We must be ready."

He paused, puffing his pipe a few times to keep its
spark alive.

"We must be watchful. Then at the Big Council we
will discuss the matter."

This seemed reasonable to Looks Far. The Big Council and Sun Dance, involving all the bands of the tribe,
would come soon. They would meet in the Moon of
Roses, and the Moon of Greening was practically here.
He rose, seeing that the interview was at an end.

"It is good, my chief."

"I send my greetings to your father and to Standing
Bird."

"Thank you, uncle."

Looks Far wound his way among the lodges in the
fading light of day. The big lodge of Chickadee's parents was unmistakable even in the twilight, with its
decoration of a large buffalo's head. A similar design
could be seen on the bullhide shield that hung on the

pole in front of the lodge. Similar insignia designated the ownership of other lodges. Looks Far noted several shields with the insignia of friends or acquaintances.

Just now he hurried to rejoin his family. Lone Bull himself answered the tap on the lodge cover and welcomed the young man inside.

"Come in, my son! *Aiee*, how the children have grown! Little Star is almost a young woman, and Prairie Dog will soon be a warrior."

The children smiled self-consciously, flattered yet embarrassed by their grandfather's compliments. The women chatted comfortably as they prepared food. The fire's warmth was good against the chill of the spring evening.

They talked far into the night, after the children were fast asleep. Lone Bull felt little threat from the invaders.

"Is ours not the most powerful band of the People? We have stood against the Head Splitters for many generations. Can these Blue Paints be worse?"

It was reassuring to hear the confident tone of Lone Bull's talk. Looks Far began to feel better about the entire situation. Thus he was ready to consider a suggestion that arose.

"Why not leave Chickadee and the children with us until the Big Council? It is only a short while!"

It was Plum Leaf, Chickadee's mother, who suggested the idea. Looks Far was reluctant at first. He hated to be apart from his family. He even considered staying with them, but it seemed impractical. Also, his father would be concerned about the results of the mission. Finally he agreed. It must be said that the thought of danger to his family had never occurred to him. How could they be safer than in the lodges of the powerful Northern band?

"It is good," agreed Looks Far.

4

» » »

The return trip was pleasant and uneventful for Looks Far. He had always enjoyed time to himself, time to think, to realign himself with the world.

On a sudden whim, he turned aside to the west. He spent a day on the hilltop where he had taken his vision fast. In another moon, the rolling hills that spread before him to earth's rim would be green with growing grasses. Now they were muted with the soft pinks and yellows of last year's dead growth.

Soon it would be time to burn the prairie, to bring back the buffalo. The summers come and go, he thought, but the hills never change except for the seasons. The buffalo, too, come and go, drawn by the rich grasses of the tallgrass hills, the Sacred Hills of the People.

Here in the isolation of vast distances, Looks Far felt the sensation of strength flowing into his body, yes, into his spirit also. He felt a confidence, a calm that seemed to rise above the troubles of the day. When he rode on, he was refreshed, and his heart was good.

The young man arrived at the camp of his own band, and released his tired horse to mingle with the herd. He made his way through the village, passing his own lodge on the way to that of his parents. The smoke flaps and the door were still tightly closed. How lonely an empty lodge is, he thought. It needs the spirits of its people to support its own spirit. It was well known that an empty lodge deteriorates rapidly. He turned aside for no other reason than to lay a hand for a moment on the lodge skin. He could not have told why.

Looks Far had almost reached his parents' lodge when a young man called to him.

"Looks Far! You have heard the news? We are forming a war party to go and help against the Blue Paints."

Alarm gripped the heart of Looks Far like a cold hand in the night.

"What news? Where?"

The story was short. A messenger had arrived from the Northern band only yesterday. Looks Far realized that the man must have passed him when he turned away on his side trip.

The message was also very simple. Scouts had discovered large numbers of well-armed Blue Paints traveling the prairie. At least one band appeared to be a village on the move, with baggage piled on pole-drags, and women and children in great numbers. The newcomers apparently intended to stay. These new developments had been startling enough to make the Real-chief notify the other bands. There had still been no overt action.

A party of the Southern band was forming to help make a show of strength. In all truth, it was primarily an exciting adventure for young warriors. It was a restless time of year, and the young men needed a diversion after the confinement of winter. The party would depart next morning, some twenty in number.

"It is good. I will go with you," mumbled Looks Far.

His thoughts were far away, and a dread was creeping into his heart. Normally he would have looked on such an expedition as youthful foolishness. Now he could think only of his family.

Why had he been so foolish, to leave them with the band nearest the danger? But no, he told himself, the Northern band is invincible. He was not entirely convinced. He hurried to his parents' lodge.

"Good!" Horse Seeker spoke with great relief. "You are safely back. You have heard the news?"

"Yes, Father. I go back with the war party."

"But why, Looks Far? That is for impatient young warriors!"

"Father, Chickadee and the children are with her parents!"

The older man took a long breath.

"*Aiee,*" he spoke softly.

Yellow Bird said nothing beyond a sharp intake of breath. Horse Seeker spoke after a long, clumsy pause.

"Of course you must go to them."

"Looks Far," his mother finally observed, "it would be good for you to stay with the Northern band until the Big Council. We can find someone to move your lodge."

After some discussion, this was decided as the most practical course. The evening was spent in making arrangements, and in preparing food for the journey.

There was little sleep that night for the Southern band. Exuberant young men called to each other, or rode horses through the camp. Tired as he was from the journey just completed, Looks Far could not rest. His mind was far away, with his family. He felt so completely helpless. His only comfort was in constantly reassuring himself that they were safe in the protection of Lone Bull, of Yellow Hawk's skilled warriors, and of the total might of the Northern band.

Even then, he was unable to completely convince himself. He was out before dawn, readying his horse for travel. He had resisted the impulse to ride on ahead, to take an extra horse and ride through the night.

Many times in the ensuing days, Looks Far rankled under the limitations of traveling with a large party. They could move no faster than the slowest horse.

Most irritating of all, however, was the joking, holiday attitude on the part of some of the younger men. They seemed to take nothing seriously. Their leader, a young subchief named Walking Elk, seemed capable enough, but his followers were so flighty, so inexperienced.

Finally, on the last night before their expected arrival at the Northern band's camp, Looks Far could take no more. The immature youngsters had gathered around a fire to one side of the sleeping area. They were gambling with the plum stones, joking and telling stories far into the night.

At last Looks Far rose to saddle his horse. A warrior of rank and file could not leave the group, but there were some privileges to his status as a medicine man.

"Walking Elk," he called to the seated subchief, "I ride ahead."

The other waved in acknowledgement, and Looks Far moved away from the night camp. He paused for a glance at the Real-star to establish direction, then at the Seven Hunters for an estimate of time. He touched a heel to the mare's flank and set out at a swinging trot.

5

>> >> >>

Even with half a night's start, it was near the highest point of Sun Boy's run before Looks Far neared his goal. His first inkling that something was wrong came with a black smudge of smoke on the horizon.

He was alert instantly. The smoke of campfires and cooking that he had expected to see would have been thin and gray-white. This dirty smear was thick, greasy, and rose in a billowing column. Looks Far kicked his surprised mare into a run, dreading what he would find. As he rode, he checked his bow, and felt the quiver behind him to be certain that he had arrows. He might still be needed in a fight.

The mare was blowing hard, stumbling on her feet by the time they topped the last ridge and looked down into the camp of the Northern band. The extent of the loss was appalling. Already Looks Far could see that more than half the lodges lay in ashes, or still billowed greasy smoke.

The high-pitched keening wail of the Song of Mourning reached his ears, punctuated occasionally by a scream of anguish. Even as he rode down the slope, fear for his family clutching at his heart, another question flitted through his mind. Where were all the people? There should be many more than this.

His vision was obscured by the blowing smoke as he approached the first of the lodges. The horse suddenly shied away from something on the ground, and the young man paused to look.

A well-built warrior lay on his back before his lodge, his body riddled with wounds. The corpse was headless.

There was a shift of the breeze, and the now excited mare jumped again. Looks Far glanced around at the pole in front of the lodge. A shield hung there, but something else, too.

It was so incongruous that it took a moment for the young man's tortured mind to grasp the significance. The head of the lodge's owner hung from the pole, tied by its long hair.

Horrified, Looks Far pushed on. It was easy to become disoriented, with previously standing lodges now reduced to piles of greasy ashes. He dismounted, the mare by now becoming completely unmanageable. He lost his way, and frantically retraced his steps. He was nearing panic.

Corpses lay everywhere, like the worst nightmare of one's life. Many were dismembered, most were headless. The black smoke shifted and allowed a better glimpse of the camp from time to time. It could be seen that in front of the lodges, the poles that had once held the shields and weapons of the warriors were now adorned with the heads of their families. Revulsion and anger rose to compete with his panic, the dry taste like that of ashes in his mouth.

He rushed among the lodges, pushing toward his goal, choking through the smoke as he searched. Here and there a survivor crouched or stood numbly, stunned by the magnitude of the slaughter.

Looks Far reached the spot where the lodge of Lone Bull had stood. There was only a smoking heap of ashes and the partially burned lodge cover and poles. He could see charred bodies in the rubble, but could not identify individuals or tell how many. Muscular limbs protruding from where the doorway once stood suggested that Lone Bull had died in defense of his family. Yet no grisly talisman hung by his shield.

"Looks Far, is it you?"

He turned to face a young warrior, an acquaintance whose name he could not even remember at the moment. The two young men stared at each other, confused and shocked. Finally the other youth spoke.

"Your people are all dead. Mine, also."

"What happened?" Looks Far's own voice sounded unreal to him, faraway and detached.

"The Blue Paints. They attacked with a small force and we chased them. Their main party struck the camp, and there were few to defend."

"Is everyone dead?"

"All but a few. Yellow Hawk is alive, but his wives are gone."

The man was crying unashamedly.

"They killed everyone. Women, children, they took no prisoners, even. They hung our heads on poles."

The heart of Looks Far sank. He had hoped against hope that Chickadee and the children might have been carried off as captives. Then there would have been a chance for rescue or ransom. Now he must accept the likelihood that the blackened bodies in the smoldering embers of Lone Bull's lodge were those of his family. In the distance somewhere, a woman screamed out in mourning.

Looks Far could not gather his thoughts, could not think what he should do. He sat down in the dust, staring straight ahead. The smoke was choking and thick, and he rose again to seek fresh air.

He emerged from the camp on the upwind side and took a deep breath. It was good to clear his lungs of the smell of burning skin lodge covers and human flesh.

A slight movement caught his eye, and he turned to look. From a thick patch of thornberry bushes crept two children. They were scratched and bleeding, their eyes wide with terror. The older child held her brother's hand tightly.

"Father?" asked Little Star cautiously. "The frogs stopped singing, so we hid in the bushes. Where is Mother?"

Looks Far rushed forward and dropped to his knees, gathering both children in his embrace. Only now were the tears able to come.

6

>> >> >>

Seldom had there been so much excitement at the Big Council. All the bands were humming with rumors of the invaders.

The pitiful, ragtag remnants of the Northern band, though now living with others, managed to erect a few lodges in their place in the camp circle. The wailing notes of the Mourning Song sounded almost constantly. Nearly every family of the tribe counted friends or relatives among the dead in the massacre.

Darkness fell, and the People began to gather for the Council. Normally the process of assembling would have been leisurely, with much visiting and social exchange. Tonight there was none of this. The People were serious, frightened, or angry, perhaps all three.

The fire was already burning as the band chiefs and subchiefs ceremoniously filed in with their followers to take their tradition-assigned places in the circle. It was painfully apparent that the segment of the circle behind Yellow Hawk, the Real-chief, was thin and sparsely occupied. Few warriors, and even fewer women and children, had survived the terrorist attack on theirs, the Northern band.

The ceremonial passing of the pipe around the circle of chiefs was somewhat more rapid than usual, but must be observed. When each had saluted the Four Winds and the pipe returned to the Real-chief, he solemnly knocked the ashes into his palm and handed the pipe to his waiting pipe-bearer.

Hardly had the object been returned to its case when Yellow Hawk opened the council. He had been a capable Real-chief, the successor to the ill-fated Rides-the-Wind, who had died after only one season. The People had become prosperous in the long tenure of the previous leader, Many Robes. In a short generation they had expanded hunting skills to include the newly acquired elk-dog. With the ability to pursue the buffalo on horseback came new affluence. Lodges became bigger and bigger, the size limited only by what a horse could drag.

Such was the situation among the People when Yellow Hawk was elected Real-chief. Their major problems had been the occasional contacts with their traditional enemies, the warlike Head Splitters. Even there, the People had prevailed with the acquisition of the horse. The People had emerged from a frightened, run-and-hide psychology to a self-sufficient power to be reckoned with. Even the Head Splitters acknowledged that no warriors on the plains were superior to the Elk-dog soldiers of the People.

Perhaps until now, thought Yellow Hawk wearily as he stood to open the council. Every person in attendance knew that both his wives and all his children except for one small girl had been brutally murdered and mutilated.

The Real-chief skipped entirely the formal introductions and reports of the band chiefs. He began to speak, with a choked voice.

"My brothers, this is the year they hung our heads on poles."

Everyone had heard the graphic descriptions of the fate of the dead in the Northern band, but for some the retelling was too much.

"*Aiee!*" screamed an old woman whose son and his entire family had been lost. Someone led her away sobbing.

"We must decide what we are to do," continued Yellow Hawk.

He turned to Walking Elk.

"Your scouts have followed the Blue Paint people. How many are there?"

Walking Elk shook his head.

"We do not know, my chief. We have seen several bands, big bands. Altogether, they may be more than the People."

A frightened murmur ran through the circle, but Yellow Hawk waved it down.

"Does anyone know their purpose?"

"No, my chief. Only that they carry their families and all their possessions. We have talked to Growers along the Big River. They have traded with them a little. The Growers are afraid, and they think the Blue Paint people mean to stay."

The murmur arose again, and Yellow Hawk impatiently silenced it. *Aiee*, why had he ever consented to this chieftainship? The responsibilities had suddenly become overpowering.

A frightened old man, a survivor of the massacre, asked for recognition and received the chief's nod.

"We must move south, away from the new people! They will kill us all!"

There were hoots of derision from some of the younger men, and the speaker looked around him angrily.

"You who were not there cannot know how it was!" he shouted.

The council dissolved for a moment into angry argument until Yellow Hawk restored order.

"Let us hear from the band chiefs."

One by one, around the circle, the leaders of the tribe spoke. Wrinkled old Small Ears, of the Eastern band, was first.

"We must fight!" he voiced shrilly. "Drive them back!"

There were hoots and argumentative outbursts. It was apparent that there was no consensus, even in his own band. But then, in the history of the People, when had the Eastern band ever approached anything in a rational manner? There were tribal jokes, generations old, about the foolishness of this branch of the tribe.

Next to speak was Standing Bird of the Southern, or Elk-dog band. He was revered as one of the first warriors to master the medicine of the elk-dog. He was very old now, and his wisdom was respected. He had taken part in the Great Battle, when the People first stood and prevailed against the Head Splitters long ago. But now, to the surprise of many, Standing Bird was indecisive.

"I do not know, my brothers. Our scouts have seen these people. They are many, and they are strong. We do not know what they want. Our old enemies, the Head Splitters, have stolen our women because ours are prettier than theirs. But these people do not steal, they only kill. What do they want?"

"They want us dead!" shouted the frightened man of the fragmented Northern band.

The Real-chief motioned him to silence.

"I do not like the thought of leaving our tallgrass hills," Standing Bird continued, "but perhaps we should move south."

Yellow Hawk was saddened. Since his youth, he could remember Standing Bird as the bravest of warriors. Now the leader of the Elk-dog band, successor to Heads Off himself, was a tired old man, who wished to avoid confrontation. The Real-chief turned to the Red Rocks band.

This branch, living far to the west, could be counted on to stand fast in their own territory if at all possible. Theirs was a fierce tie to their Sacred Place, the red rocks from which they took their name.

"We will stay," said their chief simply, and sat down again. Their territory had not yet been invaded by the newcomers.

"Mountain band?"

Black Beaver rose to speak for his band. He was the namesake son of the previous band chief, steady and well respected.

"My brothers, we know of these Blue Paint people.

They come from the mountains far north of us. They are fierce fighters, without mercy."

He waited a moment for the mutter of the crowd to quiet.

"We had hoped their thrust into the plains was only a hunting party, but it seems they mean to move here. Now we must decide. Do we fight them, or do we move?"

The question dropped like a pebble into a still pool, the ripple of whispered conversation widening until Yellow Hawk motioned for silence. Black Beaver was still standing.

"The Mountain band will stand by the decision of the Council," he finished.

Yellow Hawk must now speak for his own, the Northern band. His was the only group so far to have been attacked and devastated by the invaders. They had seen the might of the strangers. It would be useless, he knew, for any single band to stand alone. This must be a decision for the entire tribe, and no clear-cut opinion was emerging.

"The Northern band, too, will stand by the Council's wishes," he observed.

Now would someone come forward with a solid plan? He hoped so.

A young man was signaling for recognition. Yellow Hawk nodded assent, and the young man rose to speak. He was of the Elk-dog band.

"My chiefs," the youth began, "I am Looks Far, medicine man of the Elk-dog band."

It is good, thought Yellow Hawk. This one is a thinker.

"I was with the party that reached the Northern band in the time of trouble," the young man continued. "My wife was one of those lost."

He paused a long moment, and swallowed hard. The sparkling eyes and cheery smile of the exuberant Chickadee floated in his misted memory. Finally he was able to continue.

"I have spent long in visions and thought, my chief. This prairie is our home. To our Elk-dog band, the tallgrass hills are a sacred place. Their grasses grow thick in the Moon of Greening, to bring back the buffalo, which are our life."

He paused, self-conscious and embarrassed over speaking before the Council. The encouraging nods of the seated chiefs gave him new incentive.

"But these same grasses, my brothers, are watered with the blood of our ancestors, and fed by their bones. How could we leave them, to go to unknown places where the grass grows poorly?"

"*Aiee!*" shouted an old woman. "We cannot forget the bones of our ancestors!"

There were nods of general agreement, yet the People were uneasy. The rest of the simile was all too clear. How long, in fact, until those now living would join their ancestors before the ruthless might of the invaders?

"But even more important," Looks Far was continuing, "our strength, our medicine, comes from the Sacred Hills. If we leave them, we are nothing."

The frightened man of the Northern band was quick in protest.

"You can speak so, Looks Far. I say we cannot stand against these Blue Paints. They are too many, more than there are of the People."

"Yes," agreed Looks Far, "I know. And that is why we must do something never dreamed of before. We must make peace with the Head Splitters, and fight together against the Blue Paint people."

Never in the memory of those present had anyone made such a shocking proposal. There were hoots of derision and angry shouts.

"No!"

"Never could the People do that!"

"We should die first!"

Finally Yellow Hawk managed to restore order.

"Yes, Looks Far, you have more to say?"

"Only this, my chief. The Head Splitters are our enemies, it is true. But their life is much like ours. We hunt the same buffalo, we dig the flint for our tools and weapons from the same hills. Their sacred places are the same as ours! They will wish to defend them, too."

Looks Far was pleading now.

"We cannot defend the Sacred Hills ourselves, and neither can they. We must help each other to drive back the invaders!"

Slowly a murmur rippled around the circle. There was truth in what the young medicine man had said. Distasteful though the approach might be, it seemed the only way.

Yellow Hawk nodded slowly.

"Looks Far," he asked seriously, "will you lead a party to meet with the Head Splitters and talk of these things?"

"Of course, my chief!"

It seemed a simple question and a straightforward answer, but many of the listeners understood more. The Real-chief had made a request of a young man for a very dangerous, probably impossible mission.

Fully realizing this, Looks Far had answered without hesitation.

What few onlookers could have understood was that this was exactly what Looks Far had wished. He could see no other answer. After much deliberation, he had concluded that he would do whatever he must to protect the Sacred Hills, the strength of the People. If, in so doing, he must lay down his own life, so be it. He could think of no better way to rejoin his beloved wife.

7

» » »

The delegation was to consist of four, with Looks Far as the leader. He chose his companions carefully from the many volunteers.

There was Walking Elk, who had led the war party that reached the massacre too late. Looks Far had been impressed with his quiet strength and compassion. Elk's judgement, also, had prevented further bloodshed, when he flatly forbade pursuit of the raiders. Instead, he and two others had scouted the Blue Paints to gather information. This was the sort of man that Looks Far wanted with him on the dangerous mission.

Next was Blackbird, the man of the Northern band whom he had encountered among the burned lodges. This man's motives were much like Looks Far's own. He had lost his family, and had shown great strength after the initial shock. This choice, Looks Far had to admit, was largely because of the natural empathy between them. He could relate to the feelings of Blackbird because they had suffered much the same loss.

The fourth man was a young warrior of the Mountain band. His name was Lodge Pole, and his appearance made plain the reason for his name. Looks Far smiled as the young man approached. He himself came from a family noted for great height, but this man was taller yet.

"Our band knows of the Blue Paints," Lodge Pole explained. "They sometimes come nearly to our hunting grounds. Tribes to the north of us fear them greatly."

It was for this reason, the lanky youth explained, that he wished to be part of the delegation.

"I can help explain why we fear these invaders."

Looks Far nodded. He was impressed by this warrior's earnest offer to help. He had rejected several who had appeared too aggressive, too ready to anger. The chosen men must be steady as stone. Excitability could be fatal under the wrong circumstances.

At the last, he selected one more man, Broken Knife, chief of the Red Rocks. This man was a little older, and pointed out that he had often talked with Head Splitters.

It was true, Looks Far realized. Due to the customary range of the traditional enemy and that of the various bands of the People, their paths crossed frequently. No band, however, had a range that more overlapped that of the Head Splitters than the Red Rocks.

"We see them every season," explained Broken Knife. "I know some of their chiefs by name."

During the accidental meetings that happened as the various groups traveled, there would seldom be hostilities. Both tribes would have families present, and a fight would place the women and children in danger. Instead, the chiefs would exchange talk in the sign language about the weather, the hunt, and where they were intending to camp.

It was practical to do so. Each could easily find the other's camp anyway, and it was prudent not to be too close together. Buffalo hunting would be better if those who hunted were spread out across greater distances.

"Lame Bear said that they would summer at Salt River," Broken Knife continued.

"When did you see his band?"

This could be of great importance to the mission.

"In the Growing Moon. It was while we were traveling to the Big Council."

"It is good!" smiled Looks Far. "Can you take us to this Salt River?"

The other man nodded.

"Yes, we know the place. And Lame Bear may remember me. We have met often."

Looks Far could hardly believe such good fortune. As he saw their mission, the difficult part would be the first contact. Now it appeared that this step was to be relatively simple. If they could only manage a convincing argument once they had met the Head Splitters. Well, one step must be taken at a time.

"I am pleased that you will come with us, Broken Knife," the young man said. "It may make our task much easier. You will be ready at daylight?"

Broken Knife nodded.

"Of course."

Only a few gathered to see the group's departure. Yellow Hawk was there, in his capacity as Real-chief. He spoke quietly to Looks Far.

"You will give my greetings to whatever chiefs you may meet?"

"Yes, my chief."

"Looks Far," the Real-chief hesitated a moment, then continued. "This is a dangerous mission, but on it may ride the future of the People. May good medicine go with you!"

It was a long, emotional speech for Yellow Hawk, noted for his stolid silence except when necessary. Looks Far saw a suggestion of tears in the eyes of the chief. It might well be, he thought, that this is more painful for Yellow Hawk than for any of us. He nodded and clasped the offered hand in silence.

There were tears in his own eyes as he clasped the children to him for a moment. They would stay in his parents' lodge during his absence.

Yellow Bird handed him a rawhide pack of provisions, and he mounted quickly to lead the way out of the camp. Horse Seeker came up beside the horse, half feeling his way in the dim light of his failing vision.

"Be careful, my son."

Looks Far reached out to touch his father's shoulder.

"Of course."

Looks Far wondered, as he rode in silence, if each of

the men behind him felt as he did. The warm rays of the rising sun struck him squarely across the shoulders as he pointed a southwesterly direction of travel. He wondered if there would ever be another sunrise in which the world of the People could be as before.

It was either a new beginning, or the beginning of the end.

8

» » »

There was little conversation as they rode. Each man was absorbed in his own thoughts, and rode in silence.

During occasional rest stops, they conversed on a superficial level, talking of the weather and the prairie. The grasses were lush and green, and flowers dotted the landscape. Looks Far recalled how Chickadee had loved this time of the season, with blossoms nodding in the warm south breezes. It was difficult to return his thoughts to the mission ahead.

He supposed that each of the others was submerged in his own thoughts of a similar kind.

At night Looks Far slept poorly. He was troubled by dreams. He would relive again and again the terrible day in the burning village, searching for the face of his wife among those hanging from poles, yet wishing not to find it.

Once he awoke in terror with the acrid scent of smoke again in his nostrils. It was only the smoke of their own night-fire, blown in a new direction by the shifting night breeze.

He knew that Blackbird had similar dreams because he had seen the other man shift restlessly in his sleep, murmuring wordlessly while his face distorted in anguish. Looks Far realized how the restless nights were drawing his own strength, and began to doubt the wisdom of having chosen Blackbird for the mission.

From day to day, it seemed, he could see the man withdraw, become hollow-eyed and vacant. He must find a way to talk to him.

Looks Far's own problem was solved unexpectedly one night. He had walked to the top of a nearby hill as the shadows lengthened, to look at tomorrow's trail.

Sun Boy was painting himself in especially brilliant colors to return to his lodge on the other side of the earth. Against the glowing pink and orange of the western sky, the distant hills stood with warm tones of purple and blue. Soft breezes stirred the short grass. A great blue heron made his way gracefully across the prairie, heading to some distant grove along an unseen river. There, Looks Far knew, would be the bird's lodge of sticks in some tall sycamore, with his mate waiting. A lump of sadness rose in the young man's throat, but it was quickly gone. The quiet beauty of the prairie was so vast that it seemed to transcend mere human problems.

It was nearly dark when he retraced his steps down the hill. The call of night birds could be heard in the trees along the creek, and the great hunting owl, *Kookooskoos*, called his hollow song from a nearby canyon. For the first time in many sleeps, Looks Far felt at peace with the world.

He slept well, his rest interrupted only briefly by a dream. It was not a dream of terror as before, but one of peace. He stood again on the hilltop at sunset, savoring the quiet of the prairie.

Someone came to stand beside him, and he turned to see Chickadee. She was as she used to be, not disfigured by fire and death. She smiled, the sad-sweet expression that he remembered so well. There was no spoken word, but communication flowed into his thoughts. It was a message of calm and peace and well-being.

Looks Far awoke suddenly, aware of what had just transpired in his dream. Where he had been depressed and lonely, he now felt uplifted and confident. He looked up at the starry sky, and for the first time since the tragedy, he smiled.

He was tempted to wake Blackbird, but refrained. If the other man had a similar vision, both would know. If not, how could it be told? He rolled over and drew his robe around him.

It was apparent next morning that Blackbird was as depressed as ever. Looks Far decided to say nothing. Perhaps an opportunity would come later.

That day, however, he began to outline the general plan for the others. They would continue to travel toward the presumed location of Lame Bear's camp on Salt River, guided by Broken Knife. Their weapons were to be left sheathed. At any sign of first contact with the Head Splitters, they would stop and raise right hands in the sign of peace. Then Looks Far and Broken Knife would attempt communication in the sign talk.

It seemed a simple plan, but perhaps a simple plan was that which was necessary to begin somewhere.

Looks Far was disturbed that Blackbird still seemed depressed and vacant. He asked the young man directly if he understood, and Blackbird nodded absently. This was certainly not the alert negotiator that would be needed when they reached the Head Splitters.

The first of the enemy scouts was not seen until seven sleeps after they started the journey. The warrior sat on a horse on a distant ridge. This seemed to indicate that they had been observed for some time. Scouts would watch from places of concealment. Now there was only one reason for the distant warrior to sit on his horse in plain view. His purpose was to be seen.

"We move straight ahead," called Looks Far. "When they come close enough to see, we give the peace sign."

The party moved through a cleft in a long ridge, aware that on each side, right and left, a heavily armed warrior stood on the crest. They threaded along the game trail that followed a trickling stream, and into an open meadow beyond. It was an excellent spot for an ambush, Looks Far realized.

"Keep close," he called. "Now let us give the peace sign."

It was perhaps well that they did so as they rode into the open. On the far side of the little meadow, only a long bowshot away, sat at least twenty heavily armed horsemen.

"*Aiee*," whispered Broken Knife, "it is Lame Bear himself."

9

» » »

It was difficult to sit calmly, right palms upraised, while the enemy charged. It was even more difficult to reassure themselves that this confrontation was the avowed purpose of their mission.

The horses became excited, danced around, plunged and reared. The yipping falsetto war cry of the Head Splitters echoed across the little valley. An arrow rattled against the rocky hillside behind them.

"Stand fast!" Looks Far yelled.

For an instant he was certain that their mission was over, along with the lives of them all. It was all he could do to remain motionless, but any other course would have been futile. They could not now fight or run. Their trail had been chosen, and now they must follow it. He glanced right and left, and saw that the others were holding fast, also.

The charge ended only when the burly chief in the front rank yanked his stallion to a sliding stop almost toe to toe with Looks Far's horse. Dust billowed forward, choking and yellow, across the group. Lame Bear's warriors reined in, spreading around to the sides to encircle the five riders.

"Sign to him, Broken Knife," whispered Looks Far, right hand still raised.

Broken Knife kneed his horse one step forward and began the hand gestures.

"Greetings, my chief! We would make council with you. Our Real-chief, Yellow Hawk, sends greetings."

Lame Bear frowned. Clearly he suspected a trick. He turned and spoke to a man behind him, and a couple of warriors moved to gallop along the back trail. It appeared that Lame Bear was taking no chances that their main force lay behind the hill.

"No, my chief. We are alone," Broken Knife was signing.

"Why?" The question was thrown as a challenge.

"We would meet with you in council."

"No," Lame Bear gestured angrily. "You do not speak truth. The Elk-dog People do not come to council with Head Splitters!"

Broken Knife appeared startled.

"You know me, my chief! I am Broken Knife. I speak truth."

Lame Bear glared a moment, then turned abruptly to Looks Far.

"How are you called?" he gestured.

"I am Looks Far, my chief, of our Southern band. Broken Knife speaks truth. We wish to talk of a threat to both our peoples."

Lame Bear grunted in derision.

"You would help us?"

"And ask your help."

"What is this threat?"

"There are invaders from the north, my chief. They are evil, and great in numbers. They wish to kill us all."

There was a ripple of derisive laughter from the warriors behind Lame Bear. He motioned them to silence.

"No. You do not speak truth. You would not ask our help."

He paused a moment, then took another approach.

"How are these people called?" he signed with a sneer.

"We call them Blue Paints. They have killed most of our Northern band."

Lame Bear responded with an obscene gesture of

derision. It was clear that he knew that the Northern band of the People was the strongest, but he chose to ignore that fact.

"No," he signed. "No one wears blue paint."

"But these strangers do. They come from somewhere in the north country. They wish to drive us from our hunting grounds."

"How do you know this?"

Lame Bear was clearly still suspicious. He expected a trap of some sort. It was apparent that he did not believe the story of the delegation from the People.

"Listen, my chief"—Looks Far was almost desperate—"would our people ask help from Head Splitters if we were not both in great danger?"

There was an expression of doubt on the face of Lame Bear. For a moment he appeared to be weakening.

Ah, thought Looks Far. Now we may be able to sit and talk. He glanced around at his companions to see how they were reacting.

Walking Elk, at his elbow, sat quietly, ready and waiting. On the other side, Broken Knife still seemed puzzled over their hostile reception. Lodge Pole towered above the rest of the party, stolid as his namesake.

To the far left was Blackbird. Looks Far was still concerned about his instability, and now became more so. Blackbird was staring vacantly at the Head Splitters, and mumbling to himself.

This was dangerous, Looks Far realized. The Head Splitters would have no idea what he was saying, and could easily take offense.

"Blackbird," he called softly.

The young warrior did not even look around, but continued to talk, now more loudly. His words made little sense, a sort of childish gibberish. Blackbird reined his horse forward, his voice rising as he moved toward the Head Splitter chief.

Looks Far was never certain exactly what Blackbird intended. He may have been desperately trying to convince the enemy chief of their sincerity. On the other hand, his tortured spirit may have completely abandoned sanity. He may have intended to attack Lame Bear.

In any event, it made no difference. In the space of a heartbeat, one of the enemy warriors struck out with a stone war ax. Blackbird slumped into the dust. The other warriors pressed forward.

"We come in peace!" Looks Far shouted, simultaneously raising his hand in the peace sign once more.

He did not have time to look around to see what the rest of his party was doing. Something struck him across the back of the head and he felt himself sliding from the horse. His consciousness was fading, but his last thought was of failure. This had been the People's only chance for survival in their Sacred Hills.

Now, with darkness rushing in, the chance was gone. Looks Far was unconscious before he collided with the rising ground.

10

≫ ≫ ≫

The sensation that was foremost in the mind of Looks Far as he began to recover was that of darkness. Somewhere off in the distance, light flickered, and a woman's voice continually called to him.

So this is the other side, he thought. He had not known that crossing over would result in such a headache. The soft voice of the woman spoke again, calling to him in his own tongue. How comforting, that Chickadee would be here to meet him.

"Yes, Chickadee, I am here!"

"No, no," the voice said, a tone of greater urgency now. "*Aiee*, you must wake up."

"Is he dead?" It was Walking Elk's voice, somewhere behind him.

"No," answered Lodge Pole, "but he wakes very slowly."

With great effort, Looks Far tried to focus his senses. He discovered that his hands and feet were tied.

This fact drove him to another thought. One does not arrive in the Spirit World with hands tied, but free. Therefore, he must be alive. He tried to raise his head, and this last impression was verified by the pounding in his temples. The dead do not have headaches like this one.

Quickly his mind moved on. If he remained alive, and heard the others talking, then they must be alive, too. But what of the girl's voice? With a moment of

regret, he realized that it could not have been Chickadee. For a short time, the pleasures of death had appeared tempting.

He rolled over, attempting to adjust his eyes to the
flickering patterns of light in the darkness.

Quickly he recognized campfires scattered in the
night among skin lodges. One larger blaze seemed to
signal a dance or ceremony of some sort. Now his
reason, slowly returning, told him that the thumping
in his head was actually that of the big dance drum.

"Lie still and do not struggle, man of the People,"
the woman's voice spoke again, quietly.

She spoke his own tongue, but with an odd accent.

"Who are you?" he whispered. "How do you speak
our tongue? Are you of the People?"

"My mother was. She taught me."

Looks Far tried to focus in the flickering darkness to
see the girl. He could make out only a dim outline.
She appeared tall and slender as she knelt in the darkness near him. Her voice was soft and pleasant, and
sounded young, like that of a woman hardly mature.

"You will help us?" Looks Far asked hopefully.

"I will do what I can."

"What will they do with us?"

"I do not know. They think you mean treachery.
But Lame Bear will talk to you again."

Good, thought Looks Far. At least, there would be
another chance to plead their mission. Then a thought
struck him.

"The others— They are all alive?"

He dreaded the answer. He had seen Blackbird fall
heavily, struck by the war ax. He twisted his head
around, but could not count the number of huddled
forms that lay tied near him.

"One is dead," the soft voice murmured sympathetically. "There are three others here."

Poor Blackbird. No one had wished more for success
in this mission. Looks Far could feel as he had felt. It
was important to protect the rest of the People from
the fate of their families.

"Is it true?" The girl spoke again.

"What?"

"About the Blue Paint people?"

"Of course!" Looks Far snapped. "Why would we risk our lives to come here?"

Even this girl, who seemed friendly and caring, doubted their sincerity. Well, he fumed in frustration, what could he expect from one who lived with Head Splitters? He was tired and irritable and his head ached.

"I am sorry," the girl spoke sadly.

Of course, Looks Far thought. We must be pleasant to this girl. Just now she is our only hope in a bad situation. He tried to make his tone open and friendly.

"Of course. I see that your heart is good."

He paused a moment, thinking how to prolong the conversation. The girl would be more likely to help them if she felt well acquainted.

"How are you called?"

That would do, for a start.

"I am—" the girl paused as if unsure. "I am Blue Dawn."

"The name is pretty."

He could almost feel her blush in the darkness.

"My mother chose it. I—I am really called Tree Woman by my father's people."

How remarkable, he thought. Here is a sensitive young woman, raised among the Head Splitters, whose mother, undoubtedly a captive slave-wife, had managed to train her daughter in the ways of her people.

"Tell me of your mother."

"There is little to tell. She was taken in a raid when she was young."

She paused and giggled self-consciously.

"My mother always said that the women of the People are prettier than those of the Head Splitters. She told me that when I am grown, I should rejoin her people, who know how to treat a woman."

"Where is your mother?"

"She is dead."

The tone was choked with sadness now.

"Cold Maker took her, in the Moon of Long Nights."

Again Looks Far could feel the powerful emotion of

this girl, could all but see the tears in her eyes. What a strong spirit the girl's mother must have had! Through all the seasons of this girl's childhood, she had taught and nurtured the spirit in her daughter. The heart of Looks Far reached out in understanding.

"What was your mother's name?" he asked gently.

"She was called Bird Wing by her—" she paused, stammering. "By your people. She was of the Red Rocks band."

"*Aiee!*" spoke a surprised voice from the darkness. "I knew your mother!"

"You *knew* her? How is this, uncle?"

"I am Broken Knife, of the Red Rocks. *Aiee*, we were children together! I remember when she was stolen." He paused, and seemed a little embarrassed.

"I had thought of asking her to share my lodge. She was a beautiful young woman."

"Yes," the girl spoke eagerly. "Can you tell me more of her younger days?"

"Of course. Who is your father, child?"

"He is Lame Bear, uncle."

Looks Far was elated. What good medicine! Here was a friend in the enemy camp, one whose family was known by Broken Knife, one who spoke the language of the People. She could interpret when the time came for parlay. In addition, she was the daughter of the band chieftain himself. *Aiee*, how could things be better?

For the first time in many sleeps, his basic optimism was returning. Then he paused to reflect. Here they were, one dead, the survivors bound hand and foot, and their fate undecided, and their mission questioned.

Despite all this, he felt that the situation was good. It must be that their medicine was of the best. He smiled to himself in the darkness.

11

>> >> >>

If this girl was an example, Looks Far told himself by light of day, Broken Knife's childhood sweetheart must have been a strikingly beautiful woman. Blue Dawn was tall and slender, with deep, wide-set eyes in a face so gentle and expressive that the heart of Looks Far melted when he saw her.

Instantly he felt a pang of disloyalty to Chickadee over his attraction. He repressed that thought quickly. It was not an appropriate comparison. Blue Dawn's slim grace and sad quiet beauty could not be compared to the perky sparkle of Chickadee's lilting laughter, her bright quick smile.

Besides, he told himself irritably, this girl was hardly more than a child. He was not old enough to be her father, by quite a few summers, but she was more nearly the age of young Lodge Pole.

The captives had been yanked roughly to their feet shortly after daybreak. Their legs had been unbound, so that they could walk to appear before the chief. Looks Far could hardly stand. The sharp stabbing pains, like a thousand thorns of the bowwood tree, jabbed through his feet and ankles at each step as the circulation was restored.

Someone shoved him from behind, and the prisoners moved through the camp to the lodge of the chief. It was there that they first saw the girl by daylight. She stepped from the doorway of the chief's lodge and came toward the gathering cluster of people around the prisoners. Looks Far instantly recognized that this must be Blue Dawn.

She moved gracefully toward them, and he was reminded of her name in the tongue of her father's tribe. "Tree Woman." Yes, how like a supple willow, swaying in her movements as the willow in a gentle breeze. Both her names were well taken.

The girl approached and stopped at a little distance. Their eyes met, but Looks Far was careful not to show recognition. He must not threaten the girl's trust.

Lame Bear stalked over to the prisoners and growled something at them. No one moved. He repeated the phrase, and then seemed to realize. The prisoners could not understand the tongue of their captors. He used sign talk.

"Which one is your leader?"

Looks Far stepped forward, and Lame Bear glanced in surprise at him, over to Broken Knife, and back again. He appeared to believe that the leader should be the oldest member of the party, obviously Broken Knife.

"You are the leader?"

Looks Far nodded, but could go no further. His hands were still tied, making it impossible to use the sign talk. He motioned with his head toward his bound wrists. The chief nodded, and spoke to a young man who stepped forward to loosen the bonds.

Looks Far rubbed feeling back into his wrists for a moment and then began to sign.

"We come in peace, my chief. It is as we told you. Our brother who is dead meant you no harm."

Lame Bear considered for a little while, then signed again.

"I do not believe you. It is a trick. Now what shall I do with you?"

A sudden thought occurred to Looks Far. He signaled again.

"My chief, is there anyone who speaks both our tongues?"

This would give the girl the option without the

threat. She could remain silent if she or her father wished.

There was a long silence while the chief slowly turned to look over his people. He had turned back to Looks Far and appeared to be ready to give a negative answer before the girl spoke.

She shouldered forward, earnestly pleading with Lame Bear in his own tongue. He looked dubious, but finally nodded consent and signed to Looks Far.

"The girl wishes to try."

It was apparent that the chief had no idea of her previous contact with the captives. Looks Far smiled at her.

"Thank you."

Her large dark eyes, like deep pools, gazed at him with sympathy and understanding, yet a little like a frightened animal. She could be no more than sixteen, he thought. This was a big responsibility.

"Yes," she nodded. "What do you wish me to say?"

Now that they had come this far, he scarcely knew where to begin.

"Lame Bear has heard our story," he offered. "Ask him what he would have us answer for him."

Blue Dawn turned and translated for her father. This would prove useful. Though slow, there could be shades of meaning not available with the sign talk alone. She turned and spoke again, eyes bright with excitement.

"I have never talked the language of our people to anyone except my mother," she observed. "Now, Lame Bear wishes to know why you are the leader, and not this chief—what is he called? Broken Knife?"

She knew full well the name of her mother's old sweetheart, Looks Far realized, but was protecting them all. Now, about Lame Bear's question.

"Tell him that I am a medicine man. My wife was killed in the raid, as well as the family of Blackbird, who is now dead. That is why Blackbird and I have come, because we have seen the dead, with their heads hanging on the poles before their lodges."

He paused to point to Lame Bear's shield on its pole, then continued.

"Broken Knife offered to come because he knows your father, from past years, and knows him to be an honorable enemy."

He glanced around at Broken Knife, who nodded solemnly, apparently forgiving the exaggeration. The girl had begun to translate. She finished and turned back to give the chief's answer.

"Lame Bear says he understands that now. He wishes to know why the other two are here."

Looks Far shrugged.

"Let them tell him. Walking Elk?"

"My chief," Walking Elk began, "I led the party that reached our Northern band the day they put our heads on poles. I have tracked the enemy and seen their numbers. They are many, and evil."

The girl translated again, and it appeared that Lame Bear was impressed. He motioned toward Lodge Pole.

"He wishes to hear the long thin one."

Lodge Pole cleared his throat.

"I am of the Mountain band of the People. We have not seen the Blue Paints, but the River people, to the north of us, know them well. They, too, think them very dangerous."

Lame Bear stood a long time in thought after Blue Dawn finished the translation. Finally he spoke, slowly, the girl translating.

"I am made to feel that you speak truth, but I do not trust you. What do you wish from me?"

Looks Far answered, after the translation was complete.

"Only this, my chief: plan with us for the protection of this, the hunting grounds we both use. Send some young men with us to scout this enemy. Then we can plan for his defeat."

Again Lame Bear thought a long time before giving his answer.

"I do not know. I will decide before sundown."

He turned to go, then paused to call to a warrior nearby.

"Free them," he ordered in his own tongue, "but watch them. No weapons, and if they act suspiciously, kill them."

He did not ask Blue Dawn to translate, but she did so.

12
» » »

The shadows were lengthening before Lame Bear summoned the outsiders to his presence. They had spent the day in bored frustration, constantly watched by two or three young men.

Blue Dawn hovered near them. Her father had sharply questioned the advisability of this, but she had convinced him. She could, she reminded him, understand their conversations and convey any significant exchange between them.

Lame Bear was not totally convinced. It did not seem appropriate to him that his daughter spoke the language of the enemy.

Years before, when he had discovered that Bird Wing was teaching the girl, he had objected at first. His pretty young wife had insisted. It was her right, she declared, to teach the child the tongue of her mother's people.

In the end, Lame Bear agreed. He had been quite fond of the captive who had become his wife. It was with good-natured tolerance that he forgave her many idiosyncrasies, attributing them to her unfamiliarity with her captors' culture. Thus Bird Wing had fared better than many captives, though disliked by the other women for her favored status with Lame Bear.

She had been a good wife, he now recalled. It had saddened him to lose her. And how much like her was this spirited daughter, Tree Woman. Bird Wing had

had some other name for the girl in her own tongue. It was no matter. Women did such things.

Now he could scarcely believe that the child was grown, and had taken part in the council as an interpreter. She had apparently been able to speak the tongue of the strangers well enough to be understood. Lame Bear had had no thought that Bird Wing had been able to teach the child so much. What else, he wondered, had she managed to indoctrinate into the girl's thinking?

Uneasy, he kept a furtive eye on the strangers as they lounged around the area and talked with his daughter. She seemed far too pleased, he observed. Her lilting laughter sounded across the camp, over some small joke in the strangers' tongue. Somehow it did not seem right for her to enjoy the company of these, the enemy. He called her to him to scold her for her behavior.

"But, Father," the girl reminded him. "I only took them food, as you asked, and stayed to listen to whatever they plan."

"Yes, yes," Lame Bear responded gruffly. "And what have you learned?"

She shrugged.

"I have learned little, Father. It seems to be as they say."

She paused, then continued whimsically, almost sadly.

"The handsome one who is their leader is in mourning. His wife was killed by the Blue Paints. He has two small children."

Lame Bear frowned.

"That is no concern of ours," he said sternly. "You are to listen for what is their purpose."

Then he softened somewhat. This girl, he realized, could blunt his anger as deftly as her mother had always done.

"Tell me, Tree Woman," he spoke confidentially, "do you think there are Blue Paints?"

Her large eyes, so like those of her mother, widened perceptibly.

"Of course, Father! Why would they risk their lives to come here for a lie?"

The girl was using the same words she had translated for the strangers. It was plain that she, at least, believed them. But why, he could not convince himself. There seemed no reason at all that the Elk-dog People would approach their traditional enemy for assistance.

Some of his warriors already wished to kill the remaining prisoners and be done with it. It would be an easy solution. It was especially attractive, with his daughter now showing more interest in the strangers than seemed necessary.

Yet one thought continued to worry at him. Suppose the prisoners were telling the truth? For generations, the tribe of these prisoners had been the equal of any on the plains for strength and prestige. They were as strong, sometimes stronger, compared with his own tribe. Why should they ask help?

Unless, the small voice of doubt whispered in the back of his mind, unless they speak the truth. If their tale is true, there is a new force on the plains greater than either the Head Splitters or the Elk-dog People. Possibly greater than both combined.

Lame Bear took a deep breath. Could he afford such a risk? Would it be said by generations yet unborn that Lame Bear, band chief of the Head Splitters, had the chance to save his people, and threw it away?

Or worse, if the captives spoke truth, there might not be another generation.

He had been lost in thought, and was suddenly startled to realize that the shadows grew long. He must talk to the strangers again, and arrive at his final decision. Lame Bear already knew what his choice must be, for the good of his people, but he was not happy with it.

13

» » »

A sizable crowd began to gather as word spread that Lame Bear was preparing to talk to the prisoners again. There may have been some who expected, or at least hoped, that the chief would order the captives publicly killed.

Looks Far was far from pleased with their prospects. He had seen the dour looks of the chief throughout the day, as he considered their fate. It would be reasonable, of course, to send a few men to check on their story. But it was seldom, it seemed, that Head Splitters resorted to reason. "Who knows what Head Splitters think?" was an old saying among the People.

Lame Bear finally held up a hand for silence, and the murmur of the crowd quieted. He began to speak, through his daughter.

"You, medicine man," he pointed to Looks Far, "tell me where are these Blue Paints you speak of."

"We are not certain, my chief. It is said they are everywhere, like grasshoppers in a bad year."

Lame Bear nodded. He could understand this simile. After all, the problems of their two tribes were much the same.

"We think," Looks Far continued, "that their main group is eight, maybe ten sleeps to the north, and a little east." He pointed. "Of course, they have war parties spreading out from there."

Lame Bear was startled.

"They have their families?"

"Yes," Looks Far nodded, "they mean to stay!"

This was going well. For the first time, it appeared that Lame Bear was actually considering the Blue Paints as more of a threat than the People. The chief sat long in silent thought, then spoke, slowly. It seemed a long time before the girl began to translate.

"Lame Bear says we will see. Two of you will go, and two will stay here as guests."

The girl paused long over "guests," and Looks Far wondered if "prisoners" might have been a more accurate translation.

"Four of our warriors go with you. In this way, if there is treachery, they will kill you first. Those who stay here will die, too."

Looks Far was indignant for only a moment at the suggestion, and then his reason returned.

"It is good, my chief. You will see that there is no treachery."

Lame Bear then spoke again, through the girl.

"My father says that the tracker and the medicine man," she pointed, "will go. Those who stay are Broken Knife and Lodge Pole."

For a moment, Looks Far wondered at the use of two names, while speaking of the others in descriptions. But, he decided, it was reasonable. The chief had known Broken Knife previously, so his name would be remembered. Lodge Pole's name would be obvious in any language, since it formed a perfect physical description. Apparently Lame Bear was amused at the young man's name.

Looks Far then considered the chief's choices as to which prisoners would go and stay. It was logical to send Walking Elk, who had been introduced as a tracker. Likewise, the medicine man who was the party's leader.

Broken Knife, as a band chief, was the most valuable hostage of the four. Lodge Pole was simply the fourth man. Looks Far could imagine that the chief might keep that individual for no special reason. Perhaps only because he was amused by his name, his great ungainly height, and his droll countenance. Who knows what a Head Splitter thinks?

Even so, Looks Far had to admit that the chief had chosen well. Perhaps they had underestimated the knowledge and shrewdness of this dour-faced man. Certainly he had fathered a highly intelligent daughter. But that, of course, might only reflect her heritage from the People.

"You will start at first light," Lame Bear was saying in sign talk.

The council broke up, some people obviously disappointed at the absence of bloodshed. Blue Dawn beckoned them to come.

This night was considerably different from their first in the Head Splitters' camp. They were well fed, and Blue Dawn politely indicated where they were to sleep. Their own robes were returned to them, but no weapons. It was plain that they were not yet trusted.

The girl sat near the four outsiders, chattering happily and listening to Broken Knife's tales of her mother's childhood. Finally her father called angrily, and she sprang up to enter his lodge.

Looks Far lay on his robe in the soft night breeze. He stared at the sky, its vast blackness starred with points of light like a myriad of distant campfires. He marked the location of the Real-star in his mind, to establish a sense of direction before sleep.

He thought of the day just ended. They had accomplished much, considering that on the previous evening they were prisoners, tied hand and foot, with one of their party recently killed. Now they looked forward to proving the worth of a tribal alliance. He now felt that success was actually a possibility.

This in turn surprised him. Had he actually been ready to give his life in a mission that in the depths of his heart he knew was impossible? The hint of success was stimulating to his mind, his thoughts now racing ahead.

He was ready to give due honor to the girl's role in all this. What a remarkable woman! Her quiet way, her lilting laughter, above all, her understanding of the situation they faced.

His excitement over all the day's events was so strong that Looks Far doubted his ability to relax, but he soon drifted to sleep.

Once more the dreadful night-vision repeated itself. He wandered through an endless village of burning lodges, searching for Chickadee and the children. Sightless eyes stared at him from disembodied faces that dangled from poles everywhere.

The greasy smoke shifted, and ahead in the clearing he saw the graceful figure of Chickadee. He rushed forward, calling her name. She represented something sane in this insane dreamworld of death and destruction, something reassuring to hold to.

The girl turned to him and beckoned. Looks Far ran toward her with the agonized slowness of a dream, his heart bounding with joy. She held out her arms, and only then did he see her face clearly. She smiled, a quiet sad smile, but the face was not that of his wife. The woman whose arms beckoned with the promise to lead him from the horror of his night-vision was not Chickadee. It was Blue Dawn.

14

>> >> >>

The next few nights were painful ones for Looks Far. He continued to have confusing dreams involving both Chickadee and Blue Dawn. Then he would awake and experience the grief, remorse, and guilt. He was still annoyed by his attraction to the younger woman, and felt a sense of betrayal to the memory of Chickadee.

The days were spent in travel. The prairie was experiencing a good year, with adequate rains well spaced, and superb growth of the grasses. The buffalo would be numerous and fat.

These favorable conditions also made for good traveling. Water was readily available, even in the small wet-weather streams and in sparkling cold springs that could be found at the head of each gully and canyon.

The unfavorable part of the journey was the distrust of their companions. Lame Bear had chosen well. Three robust, capable-looking warriors, well armed and suspicious, seemed always on the alert. At night, only they were permitted to take turns at sentry duty. Thus one was always awake and watchful.

The fourth Head Splitter was Wolf's Head, the medicine man. His intense dislike and distrust of the entire situation was all too apparent. He was only a little older than Looks Far, but was so aloof and uncommunicative that his behavior became infuriating. Direct questions or statements in the sign talk were met by noncommittal shrugs.

Looks Far began to despair over the potential success of the mission. How could the two groups possibly establish the necessary cooperation when the Head Splitters refused to communicate?

Walking Elk was the leader of the party, at least nominally so. Presumably, since he had led the tracking party, he would have the best estimate of the location where the invaders might be found. He led the party northeast, probing cautiously, carefully scouting each ridge or hill or fringe of timber before moving ahead.

Their captors had returned weapons to the men of the People, but they could not fail to notice that they were never left alone. Even further, the Head Splitters took care that Looks Far and Walking Elk were always outnumbered by two to one. The complete distrust by Wolf's Head and the three warriors was all too evident.

Looks Far viewed the situation with increasing alarm and depression. They should be making progress in communication, should be discussing tentative plans. Instead, there was no indication that any of the four Head Splitters even accepted the purpose of the mission.

Repeatedly, Looks Far attempted to establish conversation with the dour and unpleasant Wolf's Head. Repeatedly, he was rebuffed. He spoke to Walking Elk one evening in frustration.

"Elk, how long until we contact the Blue Paints?"

"Who knows? They move everywhere."

"But we have not even begun to work together with these men. Is this entire mission to fail?"

"*Aiee*, I hope not," Walking Elk shook his head sadly. "It is the only chance for our People or for the Head Splitters."

At that moment, Looks Far happened to look around at Wolf's Head. His dark eyes were watching closely, a frown of suspicion frozen on his face.

"Look at him," Looks Far muttered to his companion. "How can we work together to help someone who does not even see the need to work together? How can we open his eyes?"

Wolf's Head seemed to realize that they were talking about him. He rose and stiffly stalked away. Walking Elk shrugged, dejected.

It was not until the following evening that a turning point came in the mission. They had camped at a spring a short distance below the crest of a prominent ridge. Looks Far climbed to the top to be alone and meditate just before Sun Boy went to his lodge. He was irritated that, as usual, two of the Head Splitters rose and followed him. He had wished to be alone, but Wolf's Head and one of the other warriors were close behind him when he reached the top.

Sun Boy had selected especially beautiful shades of orange and pink to paint himself this evening. Amid the brilliant hues floated puffy little clouds of purple and blue-gray.

To the northeast, the green of the closer hills gave way to a blue-green hue of those farther away. Range lay upon range until the farthest ridges, lying on the horizon, appeared a misty light blue, like that of a heron's wing.

Even with the enemy warriors behind him, Looks Far began to feel the rejuvenation, the spirit of the quiet hills. Their calming strength seemed to flow into his body, strengthening and sustaining. The doubts that had grown the past few days began to seem petty before the strength of spirit that emanated from the hills. Once again he began to feel the courage of conviction, the belief that his mission could, after all, be accomplished.

"I will find a way to make them see," he spoke aloud.

He turned to Wolf's Head, who stood watching him closely.

"Can we work together to save this?" He used the sign talk, and gestured broadly across the hills at the end.

Wolf's Head stood a moment, his face expressionless. Then he heaved a deep sigh and spoke.

"Yes," he said resignedly. "We must."

It took a moment for the significance of the simple remark to sink through to Looks Far's consciousness.

The statement of agreement was astounding in itself.
The crowning blow, however, to Looks Far, was something else. The three words uttered by Wolf's Head
had been spoken in the tongue of the People.

"*Aiee!*" cried Looks Far. "You speak our language?"

"Of course!" snapped the other irritably. "That is
why I was sent with this mission!"

Once again Looks Far paused to marvel at the clev-
erness of Lame Bear. The chief was still full of sur-
prises. How very effective, to send one who knew
their language, to be on the lookout for any treachery.
This explained the medicine man's reluctance to communicate at all. It would have made a slip up too easy.

"Wolf's Head, I—"

The Head Splitter cut his elation short.

"Listen to me, Looks Far. I do not like you or your
people. I do not trust you. We must work together,
but we do not have to like it. I have spoken."

He turned and marched down the hill in the gathering dusk. Looks Far stood watching numbly. It appeared that the dour medicine man of the Head Splitters
was to remain as unpleasant as ever.

Still, they could now communicate. Despite the
negative talk of Wolf's Head, the spirits of Looks Far
were lifted. In fact, they were soaring.

15
» » »

The guest-captives at the Head Splitter village suffered, too. Not physically, now. They were well fed and cared for. Their wants were supplied.

The suffering of the two men of the People was of the heart, like that of Looks Far. It was so frustrating to sit in the village of their traditional enemies, knowing that a worse threat moved somewhere out there in the distant prairie. There was also the insult of having their truth doubted. They still were not allowed to have weapons. They were watched constantly.

The girl, Blue Dawn, seemed ever-present also, drawn to the two outsiders as a moth to the flame. Her father was not entirely happy with this, but she managed to keep him reassured that she was performing a useful service.

"But, Father, how else would we know of their talk between themselves, and what they mean to do?"

"Yet, daughter, you tell me they mean no treachery."

"I think not, but should they not be watched?"

"Our warriors can watch them."

"Yes, they do so. But the warriors cannot understand their talk."

In the end, Lame Bear gave in, still marveling at the persuasive powers of the girl, so like her mother. He watched her swinging walk as she rejoined the captives.

Blue Dawn was thoroughly enjoying the two men of her mother's tribe.

"Tell me more of my mother, uncle," she teased.

Broken Knife responded easily. Long-forgotten incidents from his own childhood now returned. He told of the Rabbit Society, where the young of the People began their learning. He and Bird Wing had competed as children, he better at swimming, the girl able to defeat him at running. Not all the time, he assured the listeners, just sometimes.

"Maybe sometimes she wanted you to catch her," suggested Lodge Pole, with his droll, solemn expression.

Blue Dawn laughed in delight, but noticed the dark cloud that drifted for a moment across the face of Broken Knife. He immediately recovered his composure, and a sad dreamy smile came over his face.

"She was a very beautiful woman, little one. I missed her very much when she was lost."

The heart of Blue Dawn reached out to him, and she lay a hand on his arm.

"I know, uncle. I have missed her, too."

Tears glistened for a moment in the girl's eyes. She longed somehow to fly into the arms of this kind and gentle man. She had known Broken Knife only a few suns, but there was a bond between them already. Somehow she felt a reassurance, a closeness to her mother, when she talked with him. Theirs was a sharing of grief, an understanding of the loss felt by the other.

After a few heartbeats, Blue Dawn broke the spell. Laughing, she wiped her eyes and turned again to lighter things.

"Tell me more, uncle. What of other things in your Rabbit Society?"

Broken Knife shook himself free of his reverie, and smiled gently.

"Ah, yes. Have I told you of the time your mother nearly drowned, and I pulled her out?"

Blue Dawn clapped her hands in delight.

"No, uncle, she really did that?"

"Yes, we were maybe five summers. Some of us were swimming at an otter slide, and she tried to do everything the older children did."

He described in detail the steep slide and the plunge into the dark pool. The girl had gone deeper than she expected, and had come to the surface gasping and choking. The eyes of Broken Knife glistened with the memory of the excitement. Although there had been others present, he had been the first to reach the drowning girl. *Aiee*, how the questions of this Head Splitter's daughter brought back the memories!

"Tell me of her growing up, uncle. You said you had asked her to your lodge?"

Broken Knife chuckled.

"I had no lodge yet. I was young. We both were. But we had talked of this. I had not asked her father."

"Could you not live in her parents' lodge?" Lodge Pole voiced the question. "That is often done."

"Yes," nodded Broken Knife, "it was a thing we had talked of. But I was poor. I had nothing to offer her parents. My own father was killed in the hunt, and I provided for his lodge. My mother had three smaller children. I had to see to them before thinking of my own lodge."

The life of Broken Knife had not been easy, Blue Dawn saw. He had been successful, had rapidly risen to prominence in the Red Rocks band. Still, there must have been many heartbreaks along the road. There was one question she had to ask.

"Uncle," she began hesitantly, "if my mother had not been stolen, she would have been your wife?"

There was not a moment's hesitation.

"Of course, little one! We both knew it from the time we were small. Neither of us ever thought anything else."

He lapsed into an embarrassed silence, having shown more emotion than he intended. Blue Dawn once again felt deeply the pain that he had felt, and wished that she could comfort him.

How odd, she thought. If her mother had not been stolen by the Head Splitters, where would she, Blue Dawn, be? Would she be among the Red Rocks band of her mother's people, with Broken Knife as her father?

Or, if her mother had never been taken as a captive wife to the lodge of Lame Bear, would she, Blue Dawn, have never been born at all? It was very confusing.

16
>> >> >>

The entire sequence of events in the Head Splitter camp was observed with wry humor by Lodge Pole. He found it irritating to be in the frustrating dual identity of an honored prisoner. Yet he was philosophical and practical by nature. He was comfortable, well fed, and had the opportunity to relax, sleep if he chose, and observe the Head Splitters. It was a rare opportunity, he realized, to observe the customs of the traditional enemy from a vantage point of safety. Their customs, with some major differences, appeared strikingly similar for the most part to those of the People.

His main preoccupation, however, was in watching the relationship develop between his companion, Broken Knife, and the girl. From the first, it seemed, the older man had looked upon Blue Dawn in a fatherly way, speaking to her as a child, patiently explaining, making small jokes for her amusement. The girl, in turn, had hung on his every word, hungry for more information about her mother. The two had much in common, it was apparent, though of different generations. Both had loved the same woman, one as a childhood sweetheart, the other as a parent and mother figure. In addition, there was the strong sense of patriotism which Bird Wing had managed to instil in her daughter. It was easy to see that in her own mind's eye, Blue Dawn was of the People. All in all, this was a fascinating thing to observe.

Lodge Pole, of course, was included in their conversations. He contributed questions and comments, made quiet jokes, and gently teased the girl. Blue Dawn reminded him much of a favorite sister, at home among the Mountain band.

The young man was sensitive by nature, and his heart went out in sympathy to this quiet and serious young woman. When the tears wet her eyes like dewdrops over some nostalgic tale of Broken Knife's, Lodge Pole had to repress the urge to hold and comfort her. It was not a romantic urge, but a brotherly one. However, he thought with a wry smile, her father would never believe that. Lame Bear was hardly able to tolerate the girl's animated talk with Broken Knife.

It was apparent that the girl's father watched them constantly. Lodge Pole had mentioned this on the second day, but Blue Dawn dismissed his concern with a casual wave of the hand. The young man was not completely convinced, however. He had seen the black looks. He was also observant enough to note that their entire mission could be destroyed by so simple a thing as a jealous father.

With this in mind, Lodge Pole was careful to sit apart, at least not within touching distance, when Blue Dawn joined them to talk. He felt that Broken Knife was blunting the keen edge of his mind against his heart. Broken Knife had not become a respected chief by poor judgement. Yet here he was, totally engrossed in stories of his childhood. Surely he had failed to notice the increasing irritation on the part of Lame Bear.

By the fourth day, when the girl and the older man were becoming increasingly close in their emotional conversations, Lodge Pole was becoming concerned. He was well aware that the touch on the hand, the pat on the shoulder, between the two, were purely unconscious signs of trust and understanding, nothing more. The father-daughter relationship was apparent to him, and probably to them, for what it was. It was only that Lodge Pole was afraid that this would not be apparent to any other person in the entire Head Splitter village. He would speak to Broken Knife about it when night came and Blue Dawn went to her lodge. The chance never came, because that was the night the enemy chose to strike the camp.

It was never certain whether the enemy was aware of the Head Splitters' reluctance to fight in the dark. At any rate, they struck shortly after full dark.

Lodge Pole was stretched on his robe, staring at the star-flecked sky and wondering how to approach Broken Knife, when he heard a restless whinny in the horse herd. Instantly he was alert. There were more noises, shuffling and restless trampling across the meadow, and then the horses began to move.

They were at the edge of the camp itself, snorting and stamping at unfamiliar sights and sounds, before Lodge Pole realized that something had *brought* them into camp. The horses were being driven! If they were driven, his mind raced ahead, it must be for a purpose, and that purpose must be an attack. He leaped to his feet and ran to the nearby lodge of Lame Bear. Frantically, he beat on the taut lodge skin.

"Dawn!" he yelled. "Wake your father! The Blue Paints are attacking!"

He did not even stop to think that the first reaction on the part of the Head Splitters might be to kill the strangers in their midst, fearing treachery. He was aware, however, that his great height made him an attractive target. He had learned this in night games as a youngster.

Lodge Pole ran at a crouch to the nearest fire and tossed on it a handful of the smallest dry sticks in the kindling pile. The breeze would quickly fan it into flame, and with the flame, light. He stepped quickly to a shaded vantage point to await the next development.

There were noises among the lodges, cries of alarm as the village roused to life. The loose-driven horses stumbled through the camp, coming closer and snorting in alarm. Somewhere a man cried out, and then screamed in terror. There were other cries now.

Lodge Pole turned to find Broken Knife at his elbow.

"*Aiee*, if we only had weapons," the older man muttered.

"Down!" answered Lodge Pole. A bulky figure on a horse threaded his way along, urging the horses forward with hisses and clucks. A lanky arm reached out of the darkness, to clamp fingers tightly around the rider's windpipe. The fire flared up at that moment and it seemed that the Blue Paint warrior was plucked from the saddle like a plum from the tree, to slam forcibly into the dust. The horse trotted on.

It was only the space of a few heartbeats before Lodge Pole rose, stripping bow and arrows from the man's back. These he tossed to Broken Knife, and brandished a buffalo lance in one hand and a knife in the other.

"Now, my brother, we *have* weapons!"

Lame Bear rushed from his lodge door at almost the same instant that the main rush of Blue Paints came through the camp. In a moment, the three men were fighting for their lives.

Lodge Pole lunged, struck, pulled men down, used the knife, and struck again with the lance. He was dimly aware of two softer sounds amid the yells and screams. One was the repeated rhythmic twang of Broken Knife's bow at his left. With each twang of the bowstring, a saddle seemed to empty, its rider swatted to the ground as a fly by a giant hand.

Lame Bear was everywhere, the swish of his war club followed in nearly every circuit by a sickening, thudding crunch. Lodge Pole tried to stay near him to help fend off the rush of warriors that crowded toward the lodge. Its size marked Lame Bear's lodge as that of an important chief, and it would be a target of the enemy.

Lodge Pole lunged with the lance, missed, and dodged the retaliatory swing of a stone club. He pulled the man down and the knife flashed again.

Then, suddenly, it was over. The horses were gone, the enemy riders. Fires began to blossom, and light pushed back shadows. Wailing sounds arose as people searched for family members, only to discover the worst.

Lodge Pole sat down in the dust, exhausted.

He had seen battle before, but nothing like this slaughter. His knees were weak, and there was a buzzing in his ears.

"You are wounded?" Lame Bear asked in the sign talk.

"No. You?"

The older man shook his head. Blue Dawn slipped quietly from the lodge and came forward, followed by another woman.

"You are all right?" She repeated the question in both languages and then paused.

"Where is Broken Knife?"

17

»» »« »»

They found him in the shadows. He lay on his back, the bow still in his left hand. He had no more arrows. A lucky shot by a Blue Paint archer had found its mark. Sightless eyes stared at the sky.

Blue Dawn began to cry softly, then turned to enter the lodge.

Lame Bear and Lodge Pole looked long at each other, at Broken Knife's still form, and at the other still forms that ringed the place where they had stood.

"He was a brave man," Lame Bear gestured.

Lodge Pole nodded, still exhausted and breathing heavily.

The lodge door-skin was thrown back and Blue Dawn stepped into the open once again. Her face was blackened with ashes in the traditional mourning ceremony.

Lame Bear frowned.

"What are you doing?"

Blue Dawn did not even pause as she brushed past him.

"Broken Knife has no one. I mourn for him."

She dropped to her knees beside the still form. The moaning wail of her song rose as she yanked the arrow from his breast and threw it from her. It continued as she straightened his legs and folded his lifeless arms across his chest. Gently, she closed the eyes for the last time.

Blue Dawn paused for a moment and turned to Lodge Pole.

"Is this right?" She indicated her preparations.

"Yes, little sister, it is good."

The tears were brimming freely as her song began again, both hers and Lodge Pole's. He put his hand on her shoulder comfortingly.

A little apart, watching, stood Lame Bear. He was seldom undecided, but now was one time. He had distrusted these men, had threatened and kept them prisoner, had even killed one of their number. Despite this, and his jealousy over his daughter, these two had fought to defend his lodge, and one had died in the defense.

It was a difficult time. How could he admit that he had been wrong? Everything must be as the strangers had said, the numbers and the aggressive, evil ways of the invaders. He looked at the blue-painted face of a nearby corpse. It was true, all of it. The Elk-dog People spoke truth.

His heart full, Lame Bear stepped forward and placed a hand on his daughter's shoulder.

"Yes, mourn for him, my child. He was a brave man."

He stood for a little while, then turned to leave. He stopped, turned back a moment, and spoke again.

"Tell Lodge Pole that he should keep his weapons ready. They may come back."

He strode rapidly away to begin to see the extent of the casualties.

The sun had hardly risen when Lame Bear called the council together. The ceremonial pipe was not even taken from its case, because this was not a ceremonial council.

"My friends," Lame Bear began, "we have seen that our guests speak truth. We have many dead, and one of them, Broken Knife, has fallen in our defense."

There was a murmur of understanding.

"My daughter mourns for this man of her mother's people."

Again, there was a sympathetic murmur from the assemblage.

"We still have with us our friend Lodge Pole, who will be treated as a visiting chief."

All eyes turned approvingly to the lanky man of the People.

"Now we must care for our dead. Nearly every lodge is in mourning."

A young subchief rose for permission to speak, and Lame Bear nodded.

"We will move after the burial ceremonies are finished?"

"No," Lame Bear answered, "it is better that we stay here. The enemy would find us anyway, and we should wait for our scouting party."

There was little more to be said, and the council broke up, each family to its own grief.

Lame Bear walked back toward his lodge, wondering about the fate of the scouting party. Had he sent them all to their deaths, moving deliberately into the strength of the invaders' forces? It had seemed a logical thing, to send a probing force to gather information. Now, in light of what they had seen, the prudent thing might be to join another band for the season. He would consider that, when the scouting party returned. Perhaps they would have information that would help decide. *If* they returned, he reminded himself glumly. Meanwhile, it seemed best to wait.

A distant thump of the Rain Drum caused him to look up. Far to the southwest, towering white cloud-tops shone above a dirty gray mass along the horizon. This was good. The enemy was not likely to be traveling or causing trouble when rain threatened.

Another thought struck him. He turned and called to Blue Dawn.

"Daughter! Tell our visitor that he is welcome in our lodge."

Then, on thinking again, he walked back to where Lodge Pole followed the crowd back to their lodges. Lame Bear used hand-sign talk now. He pointed to the approaching storm, and then to the young man.

"I am pleased," he signed, "to welcome you to my lodge."

18

» » »

Seven sleeps away, the scout party camped for the night. They had seen no enemy, but Walking Elk felt that they could be no more than two or three sleeps from the Blue Paints.

They had settled into a traveling routine, and the two medicine men, while still manifesting dislike and distrust, were at least communicating more.

This night was one of more stars than there are grains of sand. They lay sleepless, looking, resting.

"The Seven Hunters are well seen tonight," ventured Looks Far.

At first Wolf's Head only grunted, but then took a deep breath and spoke. He had mellowed considerably in the intervening days.

"You call them that, too? What is your story?"

Looks Far related the tale told by the People around the story fires, the tale from Far Back Times. The Seven Hunters had become lost, following the buffalo, and had climbed far away into the sky, never to return. They had built a lodge there, and each night they circle their lodge, which is at the Real-star that never moves. In this way, they are assured that they will never be lost again.

"Yes, it is much the same with us," answered Wolf's Head.

He pointed at the sky again.

"Do you see the last-but-one hunter in the trail? He has his dog beside him."

"Yes," answered Looks Far. "Our children are shown that small star in their learning. It is a test for keen eyes in our Rabbit Society. You use it, too?"

Wolf's Head nodded.

"Looks Far, where did your people come from?"

Looks Far was startled, but pleased. It was the first time that Wolf's Head had shown interest in the other's traditions.

"We crawled through a hollow log out of the earth's center. Our Old Man of the Shadows sat on the log and tapped with a stick. First Man and First Woman came out."

"Your 'Old Man'—he is your Trickster?"

"Yes. He also made the hole where the buffalo came out. How do you call him?"

"We call him Uncle Coyote."

Looks Far nodded. Each tribe had its own name for this universal semi-deity.

"Tell me of your tribe's beginnings."

"We came from the water. The First Four Brothers came up out of a great lake. It was far away, before we came to the Plains. Each Brother founded one of our bands."

"We came from far away, too. Our people came here from the northern plains many moons and many moons ago. But, Wolf's Head, this is how your bands began, from the First Four?"

"Yes. How did your bands begin?"

Looks Far shrugged.

"Who knows? That is not a part of our story. Only—" he paused in thought. "Only, there are five bands now, but there were once six. One was lost before the People came south."

"Lost?"

"Yes, killed by enemies. That was why the others moved. But we leave an empty spot in the Council circle for them."

Wolf's Head nodded understandingly.

"You have more Big Council than we do."

"Yes, the Sun Dance is at the same time. It brings back Sun Boy's torch, the grass grows, and the buffalo return."

"How long have your people been here, in the tallgrass hills?"

Again Looks Far shrugged.

"Many lifetimes. Yours, also?"

"Yes, which were here first?"

Both chuckled quietly. The call of a night bird sounded from a distant canyon, and a cool breeze carried the smaller insect sounds of the night. It was good.

There was a sudden scream from the timber along the creek. It sounded like a frightened child, or a woman in tortured pain. Both men jumped, then recognized the sound and relaxed again.

"Spotted Cat mourns the loss of his tail," chuckled Looks Far.

Wolf's Head was interested.

"How did he lose it?"

"Old Man tricked him, in Far Back Times. Spotted Cat hid in a hollow tree, but the tree was Old Man in another form. He made a knot hole, and Cat's tail stuck out. A hunter cut off the tail to decorate his bow case."

Wolf's Head chuckled again.

"In our story, Spotted Cat sat still to trick some birds. But his tail hung down in the stream and froze in the ice, then when he leaped, he pulled his tail off short."

Now both men chuckled, comfortably relaxed. It is difficult, Looks Far pondered, to dislike a man with whom you have exchanged "how" stories.

This led to another question in his mind, however. How had it happened, when both tribes originally came from elsewhere, that both had come to feel the spiritual power of these hills? Both had claimed the area for many lifetimes.

It was not simply a matter of good hunting. Hunting was good in many places. No, there was more, something special here. There was an attraction, a spiritual tie to the tallgrass hills. He wondered to himself to what extent others felt the strength that he did in the rolling prairie.

He was beginning to think that Wolf's Head might understand. The Head Splitter medicine man had shown great insight and sensitivity in the stories of Far Back Times. Somehow he must feel the same for the hills.

"Looks Far," the other interrupted his thoughts, "are the Blue Paints real? Is it as you have told us?"

There was only a moment's irritation at such a question. Then Looks Far realized that the other was baring his very soul, asking an honest question in expectation of an honest answer.

"Yes, my friend," he said seriously, "I am afraid it is worse."

There was silence for a long time, while Wolf's Head pondered.

"Then," he stated flatly, "we must work together. You and I must be the ones to save the Sacred Hills for our people."

19

» » »

From the night when the two medicine men exchanged the stories of their people, their relationship began to improve. Wolf's Head, until now sullen and distrusting, began to relax. It was not many sleeps until the two men began to enjoy, rather than tolerate each other's company. They had much in common.

"Tell me, Looks Far," the Head Splitter asked one morning as they traveled, "how it was with your people before the elk-dogs. Your medicine men called the buffalo for the hunters?"

"Yes. Yours, also?"

Wolf's Head nodded.

"*Aiee*, my friend, a young medicine man still learns the old ways. He must learn to work within the herd with no weapons, wearing a wolfskin so he will not be seen."

"A wolfskin? That does not frighten the herd?"

"No, no. You know there are always wolves with a herd. The buffalo pay no attention unless they are threatened."

Looks Far nodded. It was true. The buffalo herds, as they migrated with the seasons, were followed by the big gray prairie wolves. Alone, in pairs, or perhaps with growing pups, the wolves were ever-present, circling the edges of the herd, mingling cautiously. They were not aggressive, but always on the alert for a straggler, a stray calf, or an animal sick or injured.

This selection of the weakest kept alive the strongest to breed next season's buffalo.

"But tell me," Wolf's Head continued, "if not a wolf, what did your people use?"

"A calf skin. We act like an orphan calf, running among the cows and calling to them. *Aiee*, I was sure I would be trampled and gored the first day I had to go into the herd!"

Wolf's Head laughed.

"I, too. I thought it was unreasonable to learn skills no longer used, and dangerous besides."

Now Looks Far chuckled in turn.

"Yes. I argued with my father, but he insisted a medicine man must learn to work the herds. I finally learned to do it well."

He paused for a moment, then continued.

"There is a story among my people about my grandfather, Owl. There was a false medicine man, even before my father was born. Our band had a white buffalo cape, the sacred medicine of the band. The false one had stolen it, and to prove who was the real medicine man, the two went into the herd. My grandfather survived, and the other man was killed."

"*Aiee*, what a story! You still have the cape?"

"No, it was destroyed when the herd stampeded. But," he shrugged, "this story helped my interest. It did not keep me from being afraid."

Wolf's Head nodded sympathetically.

"Yes. But after a time or two in the herd, the strength of the medicine is good to feel."

They looked at each other and laughed aloud. They were sharing insights they had never shared with anyone. Only another medicine man could know the triumph of learning the ancient medicine skills.

"Quiet!" hissed someone ahead.

Walking Elk was dismounting to scout ahead on foot to the top of the ridge. He handed his rein to one of the warriors. He slipped quietly among the white blocks of stone, fallen from the rocky ledge higher up the slope. The others, waiting below, watched as Walking Elk dropped to his belly and wriggled to the top to peer between stems of sumac along the ridge. He remained still a moment, then slid backward and turned to face them.

"Many, many enemies!" he signaled in the silent hand-sign talk. "Go back!"

Looks Far was startled. He was certain that Walking Elk had not expected the Blue Paints to be here. They had already probed farther into the Sacred Hills than expected.

But why was Walking Elk signaling to retreat? He looked excited, distraught, on the brink of anguish.

Looks Far slipped from his horse and sprinted up the slope, bow ready and an arrow fitted. It was well that he did so. A tall warrior rose from hiding behind Walking Elk, drawing his bow as he moved. The others were never certain whether Walking Elk ever saw the enemy who struck him down. Too late Looks Far loosed his arrow, almost simultaneously with those of Wolf's Head and one of the others. The enemy scout sank to the grass, a look of surprise frozen on his blue-painted face.

The two medicine men scrambled forward, pausing only a moment to see that nothing could be done for Walking Elk. Both struck the still form of the Blue Paint as they passed. There was a dual purpose here: to make certain the enemy could pose no further threat, and to count honors later. They wriggled to the summit of the ridge, to peer cautiously over at the scene that had so excited Walking Elk in his last moments.

Looks Far could scarcely believe his eyes. As far as eye could see, up and down the winding course of the stream, were lodges and the temporary brush arbors used by the plains tribes in their summer movements. At a glance, it was easy to see that the number of families represented here was enormous. Hence, the number of warriors also.

The effect was much like that when all bands of the People met each season for the Sun Dance and Big Council. Except this was bigger. It was possible, Looks Far estimated, that here were more warriors than all bands of the People and those of the Head Splitters combined. The situation was even worse than he had feared. They must retreat and carry the warning to all the bands of both tribes.

At his elbow, Wolf's Head exhaled a long, slow breath. The two men turned to look at each other in astonishment.

Behind them, one of the other warriors hurried up the slope to look over and exclaim in consternation.

"Come," motioned Wolf's Head. "We must be far away when this scout's replacement comes."

Quickly, the two medicine men acted. Wolf's Head sent the other warrior down the hill while he and Looks Far reconstructed the scene they wished the Blue Paints to find. The Head Splitter took three arrows from the quiver of the dead Walking Elk, and strode over to the body of the Blue Paint warrior. He jerked out two arrows and replaced them with those of Walking Elk.

"Looks Far," he called quietly, "there are only two wounds. One of us missed."

"We cannot stop to look for the arrow. Maybe it is lost in the grass."

"Yes. We must hurry."

The two men started at the crest of the ridge and worked rapidly, moving backward down the slope. As effectively as they could, they brushed away the traces in the dust, which would have given information to the enemy.

Bent clumps of grass were straightened, small stones displaced by a moccasin were replaced precisely in their former positions. No trace of earth's dampness must betray that the objects had been recently moved.

They paused to evaluate the results of their work, to judge how the scene might look to those who discovered it next. It must appear to the Blue Paints that an accidental confrontation had resulted in the deaths of both warriors. They would study the arrows from the body of their warrior, compare them with those still in Walking Elk's quiver, and conclude that only one man was involved.

Unless, of course, they found the missing arrow. It would plainly belong to another warrior, painted with his own distinctive markings.

They retreated to where the others waited, and Looks Far led the horse of Walking Elk to a clump of sumac. He made no effort to really hide the animal, but placed it in partial concealment. He tied the rein loosely to the brushy growth, and then as an afterthought tied a thong around the animal's nose. This would give the impression that a lone scout had suspected something beyond the ridge, tied and muzzled his horse, and moved to investigate. If the Blue Paints were deluded, even for a short while, the scouting party could place much distance between them.

Looks Far glanced back at the still form of his friend Walking Elk. He regretted their inability to care for the body, to provide proper burial. Yet it was a matter of survival. It would do no good for Walking Elk if they were caught. In addition, they would risk not only their own lives by delaying departure. The risk was greater. The survival of both tribes, the People and the Head Splitters, might depend entirely on their escape.

"Come on, my friend," Wolf's Head called softly. "We can do no more for him now."

Looks Far swung to his horse's back as Wolf's Head brushed out hoofprints and vaulted to his own mount. The five moved carefully away in single file.

A strange thought crossed the mind of Looks Far. Here he was among men closer than brothers because they had shared combat. Yet, a few sleeps ago, these had been his enemies, and the enemies of his people.

20

» » »

The five riders moved quickly but cautiously in single file. The warrior in the lead guided his horse into the thickest of grass, the firmest ground, the most difficult areas to follow a track. The other animals followed in the path of the first. If they could reach the next ridge before they were discovered, they might have some realistic chance of escape.

The leader headed toward more broken terrain to their right. It would be slower going if it came to a race, but there was better concealment. A thin strip of timber wandered toward the upper end of the valley, and it was toward that shelter that the party moved.

Once in the concealment of thin shade, they turned to survey their back trail. They could see the large square stone blocks where Walking Elk had fallen, but saw no activity. It was good, but no promise of safety. At any moment some warrior trying out a horse, some young couple in love, might purely by chance stumble into view to discover the bodies.

They threaded their way along the stream bed, keeping an eye to the left to locate a place to cross the next ridge. The leading warrior grunted and turned aside toward a sloping saddle. The others followed, crossing the skyline quickly one at a time. The two medicine men were last, and turned for a final look. There was no sign of pursuit.

Now they could move more rapidly, pushing the

horses for a time. Once they swung aside to move quietly through a herd of grazing buffalo. It was a small herd, only a few hundred, but the trampling of hooves after they passed would help eliminate their trail. Then they pushed on more rapidly, alternating gaits from walk to canter to trot, occasionally stopping to rest the horses.

They made no stop that night, traveling by the almost-full moon until the Seven Hunters had traversed a long arc in their nightly journey. They paused at a spring for sleep, and to let the horses graze. A horse weak from hunger was of no use, and neither was a man reeling in the saddle from exhaustion.

Looks Far took the first watch. He was far too excited to sleep. He could not fail to notice that there was no longer any question whether he was to be trusted. The others now would trust him with their lives, as he would trust them with his.

His thoughts strayed to the camp of the Head Splitters, and to the beautiful Blue Dawn. He wondered how things were going. Now there would be no question as to the honesty of Looks Far and his party. Lame Bear would be convinced beyond a doubt, and plans would be necessary for a defense against the advancing Blue Paints. Probably the safest thing would be for the two tribes to camp together, preparing a joint force to meet the invaders. There was much danger that there would not be enough time.

Now Looks Far found himself in a new position. He was concerned not only for his children in the lodge of his parents, but also for Blue Dawn. He had thought much of her lately. The difference between their ages was not really so great. He knew many men his age who had younger wives. In light of the coming alliance between the two tribes, it was not unlikely that Lame Bear would look favorably on Looks Far as a son-in-law. Looks Far was a respected man in his tribe, he had his own lodge and many horses. Blue Dawn had looked upon him with some favor, he thought. He would speak to her at greater length.

Soon his fantasies were extending to include a joyous

reunion when they reached the Head Splitter camp. Blue Dawn would be so pleased to see him. He could envision her shy, alluring smile and the excited look in the depths of her dark eyes. Yes, he would speak to her as soon as possible, and to her father when the time seemed right.

Night had scarcely ended when the party was on the trail again. For another day, and another, they pushed exhausted horses and exhausted men to the practical limits of endurance. Both men and animals lost weight and became hollow-eyed, staggering on because of the urgency of their mission.

Finally they reached an area familiar to Wolf's Head, who had now assumed leadership of the party.

"If we travel all night," he announced, "we can reach the camp before Sun is high."

It was a calculated risk. A horse might go lame, or drop from exhaustion. Yet it seemed worth the chance. They were now close enough that anyone left on foot could proceed on foot. Most important was that someone should reach the camp with the warning. In the end, after very little hesitation, it was decided to push ahead. It was a risk well worth taking.

Through the night they traveled, stopping to rest only when the horses began to stumble. Then they remounted the only partly rested animals, who groaned in protest, but proceeded until the next stop.

At the last stop before dawn, one of the warriors reported his horse unable to go on. It limped badly, even with no burden.

"Go on," he told Wolf's Head in his own tongue, adding sign talk for the outsider. "It is not far now. You must hurry."

Their hurry was quite slow by ordinary standards. Tired horses plodded ahead while tired men swayed in the saddles. Through it all, the blur of exhaustion and confusion of hunger. Looks Far kept seeing before him the smiling face of Blue Dawn. To reach her seemed the goal of the entire mission.

There were shouts ahead, and people came running. Looks Far tried to straighten, to make himself more presentable when he saw the girl. Now they were moving among the lodges, now he was in front of the lodge of Lame Bear, and someone was pushing aside the door-skin. The tall figure stood erect, and could be no other than young Lodge Pole. Close behind him came Blue Dawn. With a shock Looks Far saw that the young man led her by the hand as they came from the lodge.

His thinking, though fuzzy, realized one thing. It was fortunate that he had said nothing about speaking to her father. She would probably have laughed at him.

The fact that Lodge Pole was apparently living in the lodge of the girl's father seemed to have but one meaning. He and Blue Dawn must either be intending marriage, or already be married.

The heart of Looks Far was very heavy.

21

»» »» »»

Looks Far tried to avoid contact with the girl. He threw himself wholeheartedly, almost viciously, into the preparations that were under way for the move.

The scouts, exhausted as they were, had reported to Lame Bear, and in turn had received the shocking news of the raid at the village. After only brief discussion, the chief announced that they would break camp at dawn. It was important to join forces immediately with other bands for protection.

Now completely convinced, Lame Bear spoke of the location of the other three bands of his tribe. It was apparent that they would be of no help. The distance was too great. The Head Splitters had always ranged farther to the south and west than the People, their territory overlapping through the central plains. It was, Lame Bear indicated, as if a buffalo robe were laid upon the grass, and another spread half upon it. That area where the two overlapped would represent the choicest of hunting and of living. This was the area contested by both tribes for generations, the Sacred Hills.

Their other three bands, Lame Bear added, were far to the west and southwest. Messengers would be sent to carry the alarming news, but meanwhile, his band must join the People as soon as possible. He inquired further about their location.

Now negotiations could move at a more rapid pace,

with more trust and understanding. In answer to questions by Lame Bear, the two survivors of the People related that all bands of their tribe were still camped together to await the outcome of this mission.

"They are still at Elk River, where you held your Sun Dance?"

"Yes, they were to wait there."

The conversation was partly in sign talk, but now aided considerably by the addition of Wolf's Head as a second interpreter. Looks Far was not surprised that the Head Splitters were completely informed as to the location of the Sun Dance and Big Council. Such a gathering would be common knowledge on the plains, the largest gathering of the year.

Until now. From what he had seen, Looks Far had doubts that the entire nation of the People, with the addition of Lame Bear's band, would equal the strength of the Blue Paints.

"We will move tomorrow," Lame Bear repeated. "Will you ride ahead to tell your people?"

Looks Far and Lodge Pole nodded.

"Wolf's Head will go with you."

Lame Bear turned and strode away. Looks Far was glad to be able to remove himself for a brief rest alone with his robe. He had no desire to converse with Blue Dawn or with Lodge Pole, so he sought solitude.

When he had rested, he still avoided the two. He sought out his new friend Wolf's Head, who welcomed the visitor to his lodge.

The wife of Wolf's Head, a shy and pretty young woman, spoke very little of the language of the People. She brought food for the two exhausted travelers. They ate, talked a little and retired again for the night.

It was not yet fully dark, and the young woman moved quietly around the lodge, preparing for tomorrow's journey. She need not have moved so softly, so deep was their exhausted sleep. Looks Far, as he drifted off, saw her with a pain in his heart. Her quiet beauty was similar to that of Blue Dawn, now lost to him forever. How ridiculous, he told himself, that he had imagined the girl might be interested in him. He was glad that he had not spoken to her. She would probably have laughed. With these troubled thoughts, Looks Far fell asleep.

Morning arrived all too soon. In the semidarkness, the sounds of bustling confusion spread through the camp. Families prepared to take down their lodges and move out. Horses were caught, pole-drags improvised, and belongings piled on the drags. By the time the sun was fully above earth's rim, the first families were ready to line out on the march. There was caution, however. It would never do to be too spread out on the prairie if they were attacked. On this move, there would be no stragglers.

Looks Far carefully avoided the lodge of Lame Bear as preparations for departure continued. He busied himself with tying and retying the girth of his saddle, readjusting the bridle, anything to remain occupied. He helped take down the lodge of Wolf's Head, and fold the cover for transport.

This task finished, Wolf's Head looked around.

"Shall we find Lodge Pole?"

It could be postponed no longer. Looks Far nodded noncommittally, and they rode in the direction of the chief's lodge. The structure was just toppling, several friends and neighbors helping to handle the heavy cover. The two men dismounted to help. Looks Far found himself looking into the eyes of Blue Dawn, and glanced quickly away. He did not speak to her, but hurried to break away on their journey. He did not wish to have to deal with the situation that had arisen between them.

The three men rode rapidly, but carefully. This might well be the most dangerous portion of their entire mission. It was known that the Blue Paints were ranging far, probing into the Sacred Hills, but their exact location was unknown. If the three messengers accidentally encountered the invaders, they would have little chance.

They camped that evening, far from the slower-moving column. It was a cold camp, with no fire to reveal their position to the enemy.

"The moon will rise later," observed Lodge Pole. "Shall we rise and travel with the moon?"

Wolf's Head seemed reluctant to comment, and Looks Far was puzzled. They prepared to do as Lodge Pole suggested, drinking large quantities of water from the nearby spring. The pressure of a full bladder would waken each man long before dawn.

It was not until he had rolled in his robe that a thought occurred to Looks Far. He was listening to the night sounds, still puzzling over the strange reluctance to rise and travel on the part of Wolf's Head. The hollow call of a distant night bird drifted across the prairie, comforting in its normalcy. Then the answer struck him. It had not come to him before because there had never been occasion to think as Head Splitters think.

Now it became clear. From the viewpoint of Wolf's Head, it was preferable to avoid any kind of activity during the time of darkness. If one lost his life, even by accident, there was the ever-present risk that his spirit would not find its way to the Other Side in the darkness. Then it would wander forever between worlds.

Looks Far now remembered that a generation ago, the warrior woman of the People, Running Eagle, had taken advantage of this Head Splitter belief. During her vendetta, the girl and her companion, Long Walker, would strike the enemy by night. The People had no such qualms about fighting in the darkness. Her aggressive raids had struck terror to the Head Splitters, for her favorite targets were lone sentries in the dark.

Slowly a plan began to form in the mind of Looks Far. He must proceed with caution not to offend the beliefs of Wolf's Head. Possibly an error could damage the strength of the other's medicine, so they must talk. With proper care, it might be possible to use the differences in their medicine to good advantage.

Looks Far smiled to himself in the darkness.

22

» » »

He waited until after daylight to approach the subject with the other medicine man.

"Wolf's Head, you remember stories of a warrior woman of my people?"

"*Aiee*, yes! Crazy Woman! She killed many of our warriors. She cut the throat of Black Fox in his own bed! Her war is still talked of. Why do you ask?"

It was a long speech for Wolf's Head, indicating that it was an emotional subject for the Head Splitter.

"She is a cousin of mine. She is old now, married to Long Walker. But I thought her war might help us make plans."

"How so, Looks Far?"

"We are outnumbered by the Blue Paints. But Running Eagle and Long Walker waged a war against your people almost alone."

Wolf's Head nodded.

"Yes. They struck by night."

He looked uncomfortable.

"Yes," Looks Far pushed ahead rapidly, "and we can do so to the Blue Paints."

"No!" snapped Wolf's Head. "We cannot!"

"No, no, my friend! Not your people. Ours! The People fight well by night."

Slowly the frustrated anger on the face of Wolf's Head changed to understanding.

"And ours by day!"

"Yes. There are none better!" Looks Far agreed.

Perhaps that might be debated, Looks Far knew. The People had defeated Head Splitters a number of times in open battle with lances on horseback, beginning with the Great Battle long ago. But now was not the time to call attention to such history.

Wolf's Head was nodding, now enthusiastic.

"Yes! With a few men, we can strike by day, and you by night! Looks Far, this is good medicine."

It was difficult not to become enthusiastic now. The three discussed the use of the strike party, the specific warriors who would do well. Perhaps twenty of the best, half from each tribe, could be chosen. They could move out, probing against the invader, striking his war parties by night and day, slowing his advance, allowing the full strength of the combined tribes to assemble. If pursued, they could scatter and disappear, to regroup later.

The plan began to appear so practical that the three stopped for council. The more quickly the strike party could be in action, the better the effect. Rapidly a decision was made. Looks Far would ride on to the People, explain the plan, and recruit the chosen warriors. Lodge Pole gave him some suggested names.

Meanwhile, Wolf's Head and Lodge Pole would return to the traveling Head Splitters to do the same among that group. The two small war parties would meet at Medicine Rock, and plan further from there.

"It is good!" chortled Lodge Pole.

Resentment flared for only a moment in Looks Far. Of course, there was no reason for the young man *not* to rejoin Blue Dawn, and he would think it good.

"Yes, it is good," agreed Wolf's Head.

Looks Far was embarrassed. Of course, both men referred to the scheme itself, the strike party. Lodge Pole had not been thinking of the opportunity to rejoin the girl. Now Looks Far was angry with himself. He must forget his foolish fantasies. There was too much to do.

Yes, the plan *was* good. The specially chosen group of warriors could be harassing the advancing enemy before their two tribes even met at the campsite of the People.

They could, he thought, be like a group of wolves snapping at the heels of a lone old buffalo bull. He had seen this once. An aged bull, an outcast from the herd, was surrounded by a determined group of wolves. The great bull, even in his decline, could easily master even the strongest of the wolves. But he was not allowed to do so. The relentless gray ghosts circled and feinted, snapping at his heels, fading away like wisps of smoke when he turned. He was not allowed to rest, and this would eventually be his downfall.

So it could be in this case. The combined war party could prevent the invaders from rest.

By day the Head Splitters would strike down a lone scout here, a horse herder there, and vanish into the vast grassland. By night the People would attack any chance small party, a sentry, strike and retreat.

"Is it known," asked Wolf's Head, "whether the Blue Paints avoid death in the dark, like my people?"

Looks Far shrugged.

"I do not know. It would be good. We could worry them more."

"Yes," agreed Wolf's Head ruefully. "In Crazy Woman's war, your cousin kept our sentries in terror!"

"But the Blue Paints do not hesitate to fight at night!" Lodge Pole observed. "They attacked Lame Bear's band after dark."

The others, not having been present, had overlooked this fact. It would make their plan more difficult, but it was still good.

They separated, Looks Far pushing ahead to reach the camp of the People, the others retracing their trail.

It was several sleeps before he reached the village. He was pleased that he was observed a full day out, by a scout who showed himself and waved. Looks Far returned the greeting and moved on.

The last portion of his journey as he neared the camp, he was accompanied by a platoon of eager young warriors who rode out to meet him. They were loud, bragging, and curious, proclaiming their readiness to fight all comers. Looks Far gave them little encouragement and even less information. They would have their fill of combat, he knew, in the near future.

He must do many things before Sun Boy went to his lodge. He must make the expected call on Yellow Hawk, the Real-chief, and give him information both on their mission and on the movements of the Blue Paints.

He must call on the families of the dead from his party. Blackbird, Broken Knife, Walking Elk. *Aiee*, only he and Lodge Pole were left.

Finally, though he did not see how he could wait, he would go to the lodge of his parents and be with them and his children. Only then could he rest.

23

>> >> >>

By the time Looks Far reached the lodge of Yellow Hawk, the leaders of the bands were assembling. It would be an informal council, but an important one.

Looks Far exchanged greetings with the Real-chief, and sat down to wait. It was only a matter of moments before the chiefs were present and seated. Horse Seeker slipped into place beside his son, and gave his arm a squeeze in greeting.

"*Ah-koh*, Father," Looks Far whispered. "The children are well?"

"Yes. Your mission goes well?"

"I will explain, Father."

"Of course."

Suddenly Looks Far noticed an empty space across the circle.

"Father," he murmured, "where are Small Ears and the chiefs of the Eastern band?"

"Gone! They left soon after you did!"

The first reaction of Looks Far was anger. How utterly stupid of the band chief to lead his people away from the rest of the tribe. Only the Eastern band would do so foolish and dangerous a thing.

That thought brought on his secondary reaction. Fear. At top strength, in good condition, and with the help of Lame Bear's band of Head Splitters, the People could scarcely match the might of the enemy. Now the Northern band was at poor fighting strength and still suffering from defeat. The Eastern band had wandered off on their own concerns, lowering the People's strength by many fighting men.

The infuriating thing to Looks Far was that the Eastern band would probably escape any conflict. Their usual range, northeast in the semi-woodlands and as far as the River of Swans, was not in the path of the invaders. How ironic, that with their foolish ways, the Eastern band might be the only one to survive as representative of the People.

This angered him again. The Eastern band, object of jokes about poor judgement, had survived for generations by sheer luck. It was not even their medicine that helped. They could do everything wrong, blunder along with impossibly poor decisions, and still happily survive. Looks Far found it very frustrating.

But now Yellow Hawk was speaking.

"What news do you bring us, Looks Far? You are the only survivor?"

"No, my chief. Lodge Pole is alive. Blackbird was killed when we first met the Head Splitters, but it was a mistake. The others were killed by the Blue Paints."

Rapidly, Looks Far sketched in the details of their activities since their departure.

"So, my chiefs," he finished, "the Blue Paints are moving this way. We must prepare for a great battle to stop them. We will soon be joined by Lame Bear's band."

There was a very soft, grumbling murmur around the circle. There were still those who did not approve this alliance.

"Listen, all of you," Looks Far pleaded. "The Head Splitters are our friends. We must be at top strength to meet the Blue Paints. I have seen the main camp of these enemies. They are as many as grains of sand."

Again there was the murmur. Looks Far had not expected to encounter this doubt.

"There were five who left to talk with the Head Splitters," an old warrior of the Northern band reminded. "Now one returns. We cannot afford friends like these."

"But I told you," Looks Far spoke impatiently, "they were killed by Blue Paints. The Head Splitters lost men, too. Look, I have been with the band of Lame Bear, a noble leader, for nearly a moon. Lodge Pole lives in his lodge."

A pang of regret and jealousy over Blue Dawn was almost submerged beneath the concern he felt for his message. What if the People refused to accept the truce arrangements, the alliance with the Head Splitters? He would have to ride to stop Lame Bear's approach, to avoid bloodshed. It seemed that the situation was turning to dung. He could hardly believe that, now that the Head Splitters were friendly and cooperative, his own People were ready to destroy the plan, and themselves with it. He saw this as their only chance at survival.

"Listen!" he pleaded frantically. "In a few sleeps Lame Bear will be here, with all his band, women, children, everything. Would he do this if he meant trickery?"

He could see some doubters beginning to come around. It was true, they were telling each other. No one takes families on the warpath.

Yellow Hawk raised his hand for silence.

"Tell us, Looks Far. You have a plan?"

"Only this, my chief. There is a medicine man of the Head Splitters, Wolf's Head, who is my friend. He and I would take a special war party to delay the enemy."

He described their plan.

"This would distract the Blue Paints by night and day, keep them from resting, slow their progress until the fighting force of the People and the Head Splitters can join and be ready."

A young man of the Blood Society jumped to his feet.

"I go with you, Looks Far!"

"And I!"

"I, too!"

There was a quick chorus of assent from the periph-

ery of the circle, the younger warriors. Yellow Hawk
lifted his hand again.

"Wait!" He spoke sternly. "If this plan is done,
Looks Far will choose his war party."

"Yes, my chief. Wolf's Head and I. It is only to slow
the enemy while the chiefs meet to make war talk
and gather strength."

Looks Far felt somewhat better. At least the Real-
chief seemed to approve.

"It is good!" stated Yellow Hawk. "Where are we to
meet the Head Splitters?"

"Here, my chief. Lame Bear will bring his band
here. Lodge Pole shows the way."

"And when do you leave with your war party?"

"Tomorrow. I will choose the warriors tonight."

Yellow Hawk nodded.

"Let it be so."

He rose to signify that the council was at an end.
Instantly Looks Far was surrounded by young men,
clamoring to be chosen.

"Wait," he held up both hands to signal a stop. "I
will meet you later, and all will be heard. Now, I go to
speak to families of the dead, and to see my children.
Come to the hilltop," he pointed, "when the moon
rises."

Looks Far turned and walked toward his parents'
lodge.

24

》》》

Long before moonrise, Looks Far was at the top of the designated hill. He wished to watch the young warriors arrive. Much could be told by their demeanor, their manner of moving, their entire attitude toward this most important of missions.

He pondered as he waited. How had it come to be that he, Looks Far, medicine man of the People, was now choosing warriors for a special mission? His life had been so calm, so ordered, so very different from that of the tribe's warrior leaders and chiefs. He had never thought of himself in this sort of a leadership position. His was the role of medicine, of visions and songs of healing, of the reading and interpretation of meanings. He watched the seasons, the growth of the prairie grasses, the movements of animals, birds, and other creatures, foretold the weather, and occasionally attempted to read the future with the stones. All of this, the medicine of his profession, was very different from the role he was now filling.

He was tired. It had been exhausting to arrive after his journey and tell his story to the chiefs' council. It had then been difficult to seek out the families of his dead companions and inform them of their losses.

The time spent with his children had been difficult, too, bringing once again memories of their mother and her bright quick smile. It had been gratifying, too, to hold them on his knee, to enfold them in a fatherly embrace.

A long conversation with his father, after the children were asleep, was almost exciting in its intensity. Only another medicine man could understand the quality of his new friendship with Wolf's Head, medicine man of their former enemies. Horse Seeker nodded understandingly.

"It is good, Looks Far. You will learn much from each other's medicine."

Then it was time to go. The moon would be rising soon, and Looks Far wished to be first to arrive at the hilltop. He rose and hurried into the night.

"I will return, to sleep," he assured his mother.

The prospect of rest, even for a short while, was very appealing, but it was not yet possible.

The first warrior to arrive was a quiet, soft-spoken young man who seemed to move effortlessly and silently up the slope. Even in the dim starlight, Looks Far could see his glance move in constant search of the distant prairie. He carried a bow, which seemed to fit comfortably in his left hand, as if it belonged there. The youth nodded in greeting, and quietly seated himself on a nearby boulder to wait. Looks Far felt that the medicine was good between them.

"How are you called?"

"I am Red Feather, of the Eastern band."

Looks Far made no answer. A man as capable and intelligent as this one appeared would need no comment. Red Feather had chosen, out of concern for his tribe, not to go with the Eastern band when they left the camp. And certainly the man needed none of the usual jokes about the Eastern band.

Three horsemen were approaching now, talking loudly, bragging and brandishing lances.

"*Ah-koh!*" one almost shouted. "We are ready!"

"My friends," Looks Far tried his best to be jovial, "I am glad to see you. You are good with the lances?"

He was met with a barrage of lavish claims, and let them talk for a moment before he raised his hand.

"The People will surely need your skills this season. The part of the lancers will be the most important when we meet the invaders."

He paused, as if pondering.

"But for now—I do not know. I need men who fight on foot, quietly, with bow or knife, unseen in the night. Perhaps your skill should be saved for the battle."

The three seemed agreeable, and soon moved down the slope, still talking loudly. Red Feather said nothing, but Looks Far heaved a sigh of relief. He certainly did not need any flamboyant thrill-seekers on this sensitive mission.

The process continued. Some were turned back because of their preference for weapons, some because of their families' need. There were some who simply had been too noisy in their approach, or who failed to sweep their glance around the area before sitting. Two from the Mountain band were chosen largely because Lodge Pole had specifically mentioned them.

By the time the huge red disc of the moon had risen above the earth's rim and started to pale to orange, the picked war party was complete. There were fourteen in all, counting Looks Far himself.

"Now go, rest, and we start at daylight."

Quietly the group scattered. It was with great satisfaction that Looks Far watched them melt away into the darkness. These were men who would understand the purpose of the war party, and would carry it out with deadly efficiency. Satisfied, Looks Far made his way down the hill to his parents' lodge to seek his robe and his long-delayed rest. Tomorrow they would start for Medicine Rock.

25

>> >> >>

Three warriors of the People crept quietly toward the horse herd. It was dark, the dim starlight barely making it possible to find one's way. They kept low to the ground to eliminate the risk of being seen against the only slightly lighter sky.

Looks Far and his war party had traveled early, fast, and long to reach Medicine Rock in three sleeps, arriving before those warriors from Lame Bear's band. Once joined, they initiated their strategy immediately.

Probing the area, scouts had located a war party of Blue Paints, and were watching them closely. There were perhaps twenty enemy warriors, well armed and effective-looking. This might be a good opportunity to initiate the strike plan.

Consequently, the "night force" of the People were moving to the attack. Looks Far and Lodge Pole would drive away the horse herd, while Red Feather quieted the sentry. Then, when the sleeping Blue Paints rose to pursue their horses, the bowmen of the People would shoot from hiding places in the gully, cutting down the enemy as they ran past.

Now the three approached the herd, after waiting for the others to reach position.

"There is the sentry!" Red Feather whispered.

A tall warrior lounged carelessly against a rocky outcrop, halfheartedly watching the dim shapes of grazing animals. Red Feather started to creep forward while the others made ready to approach the horses. The sentry yawned sleepily, bored by his duty. Looks Far wondered if the man wished for the comfort of his lodge, the warmth of his woman near him.

Suddenly a cough sounded in the darkness to their right, beyond the horses. The would-be attackers instantly froze, motionless in the dark. Red Feather scuttled back to them.

"What is it?" he whispered.

"I do not know."

"Another sentry?"

"Maybe."

The three strained their eyes into the gloom, waiting. The cough came again, then the sound of a man clearing his throat to spit. The sounds seemed to come from the area of a couple of small trees across the meadow. They glanced back at the bored lookout against the rock. He must have heard, but took no notice. There was only one conclusion. This man was aware of the other, and of his location.

"There are two sentries," Lodge Pole voiced the thoughts of all. "I will go around and take the other. When he is down, I will give the call of *Kookooskoos*, the owl. Then I will start to drive the horses, that way."

He pointed to a distant hill. Looks Far nodded.

"It is good. Red Feather, be ready to shoot this sentry when the owl calls."

Lodge Pole had already vanished into the darkness, and the others moved out. Looks Far slipped quietly among the horses, looking for one with a willing disposition. All would be good mounts. One does not take a poor horse on a war party. It remained only to find one that would remain calm until the right moment.

He selected a stocky mare, slipped a thong around her neck, and knotted the magic circle of the war bridle around her lower jaw. Then he turned to watch and wait. The sentry still lounged against his rock, dimly seen against the scatter of stars at the horizon.

At that moment the soft mysterious cry of an owl floated across the meadow. The sentry became alert, sensing something wrong. There should be no owl in the tree where his comrade sat. It was only the space of a heartbeat before a bowstring twanged, and the figure of the sentry slid quietly to the ground.

Looks Far swung to the mare's back, just as Red Feather voiced the deep, full-throated war cry of the People, the signal to alert the bowmen in the gully.

There were shouts and cries of alarm from the sleeping area near the fires. Men came running. Looks Far was already rounding up the horses, pushing, shouting, swinging his rope. He could hear Lodge Pole on the other side.

The shouts were nearer now, men calling to one another as they ran. It should be nearly time—now! The moment was unmistakable when the People loosed their barrage of arrows at the Blue Paints. Shouts of alarm turned to screams of pain and cries of warning.

Looks Far imagined he could hear the deadly twanging as the second volley was loosed. There were more screams, more confusion.

Now the horse herd was moving. He could see Lodge Pole working his way toward him, calmly urging his horse along, pushing loose horses ahead. They bunched the animals and urged them out onto the open plain. Their companions would scatter and make their way to a meeting point.

There was to be no combat beyond the initial volleys in the dark. The People would fade away, into the night. The enemy would not pursue unknown attackers into the darkness. Any of the People who for any reason could not reach the meeting place would make their way alone back to the hidden camp at Medicine Rock. Any who failed to appear would be considered dead.

Behind him, Looks Far heard the fading sounds of the enemy camp. The frantic screams had subsided, replaced by urgent calls to missing comrades, and the moaning cries of the wounded.

The horses were moving well, and Lodge Pole moved his horse nearer to that of Looks Far as they continued to push the herd along.

The two rode in silence for a little while, and then Lodge Pole spoke in wry comment.

"Tonight, my friend, the Blue Paints will know that they have met the People."

26

>> >> >>

Dawn was breaking before the last of the raiding party straggled into the camp at Medicine Rock. There was much excitement, with men who could not speak each other's language warmly congratulating the success of the foray. There had been no casualties among the People, except for Red Dog's skinned knee. He had run into a rock in the dark.

There was some question what to do with the captured horses. There were twenty-one of them, some of excellent quality. Several warriors exchanged their own mounts for a favored animal.

It was decided to keep the herd nearby. In an emergency they could always be abandoned. Meanwhile, the enemy war party was thought to be on foot.

This was verified by a scout who jogged in to report. The Blue Paint party apparently had only one horse left. As soon as it was light, a warrior rode off in great haste to the north, presumably to carry the news of the attack to the main camp.

"What are the rest doing?"

The question was asked by Wolf's Head.

"Traveling on foot, in the same direction. There are eleven or twelve, several with wounds."

"Then we should strike them before the rider returns with help."

Men were swinging to the backs of their horses,

readying weapons. The messenger would not return for maybe two sleeps, but why take chances?

Looks Far stepped alongside the horse of Wolf's Head.

"May your medicine work as well as ours last night, my friend!"

Wolf's Head smiled and nodded. His Head Splitter warriors were ready and eager.

"You will not try to stop the rider?" Looks Far asked.

"Ah, we think the same," Wolf's Head smiled. "He must carry the message to his people!"

"Yes. They must have doubts."

"We will give them doubts!"

He wheeled his horse and led his warriors at an easy lope toward the enemy.

Looks Far watched them go, wondering to himself at the progression of events. Neither he nor Wolf's Head were basically warriors. Their interests and skills were along other paths. Yet here were the two of them, peaceable medicine men, leading a war party of skilled fighters. Wolf's Head, he knew, felt as he did. Only the threat to the survival of their people could induce the two of them to follow this path.

It was nearly midday when Wolf's Head and his warriors knelt just below the crest of a ridge and watched the Blue Paints below. The survivors of the night raid were moving as rapidly as possible on foot, half carrying their wounded. They were far from the arrogant invaders they had once been. For a moment Wolf's Head felt a pang of sympathy for the defeated war party.

Then a more practical thought displaced his sympathy. Any one of the warriors below would happily kill men, women, or children. They had demonstrated this already. To destroy these invaders would be no different than to kill a real-snake that crawls under the lodge cover. He slid back down the slope and motioned his warriors to him.

"You see our mission. They number one or two more than we do, but some are wounded."

"We attack them in the open?"

"No. We would have injuries. We ride around them, hide in the trees along the stream, and kill them as they approach."

"We leave one or two to carry the tale?"

"Yes. Spare the ones with the worst wounds, and one able-bodied man."

"Why, Wolf's Head?"

"It takes someone to care for wounded. That takes another out of action. The able-bodied one is to make sure the rest learn of this."

The warriors mounted and rode to the right, along the ridge, but below its crest. They would ride long and hard to avoid being seen, and hide at the distant stream before the enemy party arrived.

They skirted the end of the ridge and dropped behind an intervening hill to move northward, parallel to the Blue Paints' line of march. When they arrived at the stream, they hurried along in the concealment offered by the fringe of timber. Horses were concealed in a dense thicket, each muzzle tied with a thong to keep the animals from crying out. One man would stay with the horses. The others scattered quickly to find advantageous places of concealment.

There was little question where the enemy would approach the stream. A game trail meandered down the slope, trodden deeply into the sod by untold generations of buffalo and elk. Such a trail always followed the easiest course, so it was used by both animal and human inhabitants of the prairie.

The followers of Wolf's Head were scarcely hidden when the first Blue Paint warrior appeared. He was perhaps two bowshots away. The man paused, studied the terrain carefully, and proceeded down the slope. The others followed.

The Blue Paints had contrived a sort of pole-drag for one of the wounded. Two of the others pulled it along behind them. Ah, yes, Wolf's Head saw. That would be the wounded man they should spare. He was undoubtedly in good enough condition to survive, but badly enough injured to require much care. Wolf's Head whispered to the men on each side of him.

"Spare the one on the pole-drag, and one who pulls him."

The word was passed up and down the line, as hidden warriors fitted arrows to bows. The Blue Paints progressed slowly down the slope, following the game trail, now apparently unsuspecting.

There was a moment at the last when Wolf's Head felt again a twinge of sympathy for the Blue Paints. It lasted only a moment, before he loosed his arrow at the warrior in the lead.

"Now!" he called as the missile flew on its way.

Like a swarm of angry yellow jackets the cluster of deadly arrows flitted across the slope. Men paused in midstride, dropped in their tracks, or tried to run, hampered by their wounds. One screamed. One man, unscathed in the first volley, attempted to retreat. An arrow reached out, arching high, to strike him down.

One of the men pulling the pole-drag fell like a stone. The other dropped his side of the drag and knelt to ready his bow for defense.

In the space of a few heartbeats it was all over. The men of Wolf's Head's party moved among the dead and dying, counting honors here and there, using the stone war clubs that gave their tribe its name.

The man crouched by the fallen pole-drag loosed one arrow, but the warrior for whom it was intended stepped nimbly aside in mock terror. Everyone else laughed. The Blue Paint rose, cast his bow aside, and motioned to his breast.

"Kill me!" he motioned in sign talk. "I am disgraced!"

Everyone laughed again, and Wolf's Head stepped forward.

"No," he signaled. "You must tell your people what has happened. These are our hills. Go back where you came from!"

The Blue Paint drew himself up, proudly.

"My people go where they wish. The wolves will gnaw your bones, dung-eater!"

"Tell that to your friends," Wolf's Head pointed to the still forms in the grass.

He turned, deliberately placing his back to the Blue Paint as he strode away. The others would be on guard for any treacherous move, but there was none.

Some of the warriors retrieved their arrows, but most left them, a personal message to the enemy.

It is good, thought Wolf's Head. The Blue Paints, when they see the pattern of the arrow, will realize that this attack is by a different tribe than the one who struck them in the night. This might even discourage their invasion of the tallgrass hills.

In his heart, Wolf's Head knew that it would not. So mighty a force as the Blue Paints would not be dissuaded by a few shots in the dark, or an ambush by a handful of warriors.

The worst, he was certain, was yet to come. In fact, this affront might well bring the massed might of the Blue Paints down upon their heads.

27

>> >> >>

The men of the combined war party understood the hazards of their mission. At any time they must be prepared to scatter if the Blue Paints threatened in force. Still, the initial success of their first combat was exhilarating. The prestige of their leaders rose, and with it the confidence of all concerned. The mission, begun almost in desperation, now showed indications of success.

True, in calmer, more reasonable moments, each man suspected that their prospects were very questionable. As soon as their plan was realized by the Blue Paints, larger forces would come.

With these thoughts in mind, Looks Far and Wolf's Head kept scouts constantly probing toward the enemy. They were to avoid contact at all costs, and only to keep the war party advised of the enemies' actions.

It was in this manner that they learned of the approach of the enemy war party. A group of about twenty Blue Paints, riding hard, were approaching from the north. It appeared that this was a vengeance raid, a response to the destruction wrought by the combined strike force.

The size of the approaching Blue Paint group also indicated their arrogance. In the confidence of strength, the enemy was throwing a comparatively small force against those who had struck from ambush in the dark.

Now was the time to follow the prearranged plan. They would abandon the temporary camp at Medicine Rock, and scatter, to reassemble later. Men busied themselves with preparations, and an assembly point was agreed upon. The enemy party was expected before evening.

There was some regret on the part of the warriors. Many would have preferred to stay and fight.

"We could defeat them," observed one warrior. "They have no more than we."

It was tempting, but not according to plan. In addition, it was dangerous. There were certain to be casualties, in an equally matched conflict. Even if they succeeded in stopping the invaders' war party, it would be at considerable loss. They could not afford to lose these, the best warriors of both their tribes, with the expectation of a massed battle in the near future. Both Looks Far and Wolf's Head were agreed. It was not a risk they were willing to take.

"But they think they outnumber us," Lodge Pole observed quietly. "We could trick them."

"No," insisted Looks Far. "The risk is too great."

"Wait, my friend," Wolf's Head spoke thoughtfully. "Lodge Pole speaks truth. They have not yet reasoned that two different war parties struck them. Each of their survivors speaks of perhaps ten warriors."

"Yes!" added Lodge Pole. "That is why they send only twenty against us."

"My friend," Wolf's Head spoke, "do you remember the story of the first battle on horseback between our people?"

"Yes," Looks Far nodded, "we call it the Great Battle."

"Great for you, yes," responded the Head Splitter ruefully. "For us, a defeat. But do you remember how your people tricked us?"

Looks Far had heard the story many times. By prearranged plan, a few young men had shown themselves to the enemy and had then retreated. The Head Splitters, in hot pursuit, had blundered into an ambush set up by Heads Off, great-grandfather of Looks Far. It was

the first major defeat of Head Splitters by the People.
Of course, Looks Far knew the story well.

"We could send a few warriors out to lead them
here," Wolf's Head was continuing. "They would expect no more."

It took a moment for the possibilities to be realized.
The Blue Paints expected to be chasing no more than
eight or ten men. No sign of a larger camp would be in
evidence, since they had had no fires and had kept the
horses concealed.

"Yes!" Looks Far now saw the possibilities. "It is
good!"

Quickly, plans were completed. Eight warriors, under leadership of Lodge Pole, set out to meet the
invaders while the others began to prepare the reception. The horses must be carefully hidden, the bowmen deployed, before the arrival of the Blue Paints.

"Here they come!"

The wait had been long for Lodge Pole and his
party. They had begun to think that they had missed
the invaders. They were waiting on a hilltop, watching northward, near the site of the second skirmish.
Lodge Pole was anxious. Sun Boy was far past overhead. If the enemy did not appear soon, there was not
time to carry out their plan before dark. And by this
time the People were beginning to think in terms of
their allies' religious customs. It would not do to force
the Head Splitters to fight in the darkness.

Now the scene must be just right. The Blue Paints
must be duped into pursuit.

"We will show ourselves there," Lodge Pole pointed
to an open grassy hilltop.

It would be a little time before the approach of the
enemy. They rode to the meadow below the hilltop,
and spread out as if traveling. Then, very deliberately,
they ascended the slope at an angle, to appear to be
crossing the path of the oncoming invaders.

Cautiously they watched the reactions of the Blue
Paints in the distance. It would be all-important now
to be convincing. Just the right amount of apparent

fear, of retreat in mock consternation. They must time their speed in flight, careful not to completely outdistance their pursuers.

Now the Blue Paints pushed forward, pointing to the fleeing party in the distance. Lodge Pole shouted in terror, and with the others, wheeled to retreat.

Straight across the open grassland they sped, over the next rise and on, fleeing for their lives. One rider waited in concealment until he was certain that the Blue Paints still pursued. Then he mounted and galloped to overtake the others.

Across the next range of hills the chase continued. Once they paused and waited for the Blue Paints, making certain that it did not appear so. The invaders, bent on vengeance, were punishing their already tired horses, hoping to close the intervening distance.

Now they drew nearer, tasting success as their quarry fled before them. It seemed to the pursuers that in their terror, the warriors ahead were becoming desperate. Their horses slid down a rocky slope and splashed across a stream to gallop toward a thin strip of timber ahead.

It appeared almost stupid, in the lengthening shadows, for the fleeing war party to seek shelter there. The Blue Paint leader put his horse down the slope, followed closely by the others. They clattered across the rocky gravel bar and turned toward the thin band of trees. The last of the fleeing warriors ahead was just ducking into concealment.

Spread in a frontal charge, the Blue Paints thundered among the trees, seeking targets for bow and ax. There appeared no way that their quarry could escape across the stream, which widened appreciably at this point. Those who were not killed in the trees would be forced into the open again, to be hunted down as they ran.

Suddenly the entire scene changed. Their apparently desperate victims turned to defend themselves. At almost the same moment, the air was filled with the dull buzz of well-aimed arrows.

The last sight that many of the Blue Paints saw that

day at Medicine Rock was that from every willow bush along the stream suddenly sprouted a determined warrior with bow drawn.

The last sound that they heard was the high-pitched yipping war cry of the Head Splitters, mingled with the deep-throated yell of the People.

28

>> >> >>

The two medicine men talked long that night. Their success so far had raised morale to extremes not seen before. The war party had killed forty of the enemy invaders, and had captured nearly as many horses.

They had lost only two men, with three more slightly wounded, in the skirmish by the river.

Still, it was now time to move. Both men felt that the invaders would be increasingly determined to punish the raiding party that was causing their problems. Their general area of operations was now known, and future activities on the part of the Blue Paints would be in great force. They must fall back and establish a new camp for the strike party.

They could continue their delaying action, harassing the enemy, but their surprise factor was now gone. The invader would be on guard.

The two leaders agreed that their combined tribes should be informed of current developments. Messengers could go, taking the captured horses as evidence of success.

After further talk, Looks Far and Wolf's Head decided to take the task themselves. Each could report in detail to his chief, and ask directly as to the progress of the fighting force preparing to meet the enemy. More and more, it seemed inevitable that a huge battle would occur before the Moon of Ripening.

Meanwhile, Lodge Pole would move the war party

to a selected campsite on Sycamore River. He would continue to scout the movements of the enemy.

One last decision occurred at the request of Red Feather.

"My friends, I know a great battle is coming. I would go to bring help from my band."

Red Feather had been, they knew, sensitive about the Eastern band's defection. No one thought the less of Red Feather, but he seemed personally concerned that the Eastern band uphold its duty to the tribe.

"I know many warriors who will return," he promised.

"It is good, my brother," Wolf's Head spoke. "They will be needed when we meet the Blue Paints."

Red Feather left before dawn, traveling alone. Looks Far felt certain of the success of the man's mission, so sincere was his approach.

Shortly after daylight, the entire war party was on the move. The other warriors helped to round up the captured horses and start them on the way. Soon they parted company, Lodge Pole with the war party toward their new camp, and the two medicine men driving the horse herd. Lodge Pole rode alongside Looks Far for a little way before they parted.

"My friend," the tall warrior began hesitantly, "will you do a thing for me?"

"Of course."

"Would you go and talk to Blue Dawn?"

Looks Far was uncomfortable, but realized it was a reasonable request. It was natural for a man to send a message to his family. But why not send it by Wolf's Head, who would be in the lodge of Blue Dawn's father anyway?

"What do you wish me to say?"

This was a very clumsy situation. He wished that he had not agreed to carry the greeting. Lodge Pole stared at him quizzically a moment.

"Why, tell her of our mission. Whatever comes to mind."

Resigned, Looks Far sighed.

"I will tell her you are well."

Lodge Pole shrugged.

"Yes, of course."

Somehow, as they parted, Looks Far had the feeling that he had missed something in the conversation.

Then he and Wolf's Head parted from the group, herding the loose horses ahead toward Elk River. The others turned aside toward the Sycamore.

By pushing when possible, and resting frequently, the two medicine men reached the main camp in two sleeps. They were met by enthusiastic young men and a contingent of barking dogs. Since they drove many horses, there must have been a victory, and the young warriors enthusiastically welcomed them with songs and war cries. Looks Far shook his head sadly.

"They will have their chance."

The two men turned the horses over to some eager warriors, and separated to report to their chiefs.

The cover of Yellow Hawk's lodge had been rolled up at the bottom to allow the summer breeze to cool the dwelling.

Looks Far tapped on the lodge skin and called out.

"*Ah-koh*, uncle, it is Looks Far."

A woman lifted the door-skin and motioned him inside. Apparently he was expected. The Real-chief reclined on a thick pallet of robes, leaning against his willow back-rest.

"Yes, my son, you bring news?"

Looks Far nodded in respect, then plunged immediately ahead.

"We have met the Blue Paints three times, my chief, and have counted many honors, captured many horses."

He filled in details, pausing to answer specific questions by the Real-chief.

"It is good, Looks Far."

"Yes, my chief, but the worst is ahead. Already they seek vengeance. They will send warriors against us that are more than grains of sand."

Yellow Hawk gave a deep sigh.

"I know, my son, and my heart is heavy. I have seen their strength. Can the People stand before them?"

Of course, thought Looks Far. No one is in a better position to know the might of the invaders than this man. He saw his great Northern band nearly wiped out.

"We must try, my chief. Wolf's Head, of our new allies, has strong medicine. We will work together, try to slow the enemy."

"But what then? There must be a big battle, and we will be outnumbered."

Looks Far had no answer. He had not expected this gloom on the part of the Real-chief. He could understand the reasons, but it was not good. Warriors do not fight well when their leaders have no confidence.

"Red Feather has gone to bring back warriors from the Eastern band," Looks Far offered the only encouragement he could think of.

The Real-chief sighed again.

"Ah, yes, but what difference will a handful of men make? And of the Eastern band? *Aiee!*"

He threw up his hands in despair.

"My chief," Looks Far tried to sound convincing, "our hearts are good, and our medicine is strong. We will fight for our Sacred Hills."

"Yes, my son," Yellow Hawk smiled a tired smile. "We must believe this."

Looks Far left the lodge, his heart heavier than before. He made his way to the Head Splitter camp, to the west of the People's village. He must carry the message of Lodge Pole, distasteful though it might be.

Wolf's Head was still in the lodge of Lame Bear. Looks Far was ushered inside, where the chief nodded in greeting.

"Lame Bear has sent word to our other bands to bring warriors," Wolf's Head informed him. "They may arrive in time to help."

Looks Far glanced around the lodge, and his eyes met those of Blue Dawn. The girl sat to one side, gazing at him quietly. He nodded, embarrassed. What an awkward situation. Why had Lodge Pole asked him to do such a thing? Wolf's Head could have easily taken the greeting, and news of Lodge Pole, when he came to report the war party's actions to Lame Bear.

"Lodge Pole sends his greeting," he blurted to the girl. "He is well."

She smiled and nodded, appearing ill at ease.

"I will tell him you are well, also?"

"Of course."

Blue Dawn still seemed uncomfortable. He made small talk with the chief, and as soon as possible, excused himself. Wolf's Head left the lodge, also, and the two walked in silence a few steps. Wolf's Head spoke first.

"What was that with the girl about Lodge Pole?"

"It is nothing. He sent a message," Looks Far snapped.

The other man realized that there was more, somehow. He also sensed that this was no time to approach the subject, with Looks Far in the blackest of moods. They parted, Wolf's Head to his own lodge, and Looks Far to that of his parents.

As he walked through the gathering darkness, his thoughts were not on the great problems of his people. They were on the sparkling dark eyes of Blue Dawn, and her sad-sweet smile in the dusk of the lodge. She was even more beautiful than he remembered.

29

Looks Far and Wolf's Head rode for some time in silence. The Head Splitter was well aware that something was wrong. He suspected that it had to do with the girl, but some things are better unsaid.

So they rode. It was a fine, cool morning, with just the crisp promise of coming autumn. By midday, it would be uncomfortably hot, but now, it was good for traveling. The horses stepped out eagerly, scattering bright beads of dew from the grass. The prairie fairly sang with the voices of birds proclaiming their nesting territory.

A band of elk lifted their heads to stare curiously as they passed. One magnificent bull, his antlers still plump and fuzzy, shook his head at them in a veiled threat. Both men smiled. The great antlers were useless now. In a few moons, they would be dangerous weapons, hardened to the consistency of flint and polished until they shone. For now, they were worse than useless. Even at this distance, the riders could see the tormenting flies that bit and sucked blood from the tender, growing antlers.

They stopped near midday, pausing to water the horses and rest a little. A great blue heron, startled from his fishing, rose in dignified flight to look for other streams, less disturbed.

"Looks Far, we must plan."

Wolf's Head was becoming concerned. His companion had said hardly a word all morning, and now only nodded with a noncommittal grunt. It was unlike Looks Far to be so.

Perhaps, thought Wolf's Head, he is grieving. He has spent the night with his parents and his children. It would be a sad thing, the loss of the mother of his children. But he should be past the time of mourning. Looks Far had acted very strangely since they left their war party.

Again Wolf's Head puzzled over the other man's reaction to the girl, Blue Dawn. Looks Far must look upon her with much favor, and it was plain that the girl returned the feeling.

So what was the problem? Had they had a disagreement? If so, when? There had been little chance to see each other, scarcely long enough for a misunderstanding. It was very confusing. His one attempt to inquire had been met with irritation.

Well, so be it, thought Wolf's Head. I will not bother him with that.

But they must talk. They must plan, must decide how best to use their medicine for the good of their people.

He tried again.

"Shall we travel tonight, to reach the others, or stop to sleep?"

Looks Far shook his head as if awakening, and looked dully at his companion.

"I am sorry, my friend, I was thinking of other things."

Wolf's Head refrained from comment. At least the other man was talking now. Perhaps he could prolong the conversation.

"You have brought your medicine?"

"Yes. You have, also?"

This was useless talk. Each knew that the other had a medicine bag tied behind his saddle. However, neither had "made medicine," had undertaken their rituals, since the war party began. There had been little time, with the urgency of the skirmishes with the Blue Paints. Now, very soon, they must make medicine.

"The moon is almost new tonight," suggested Wolf's Head. "Shall we stop early for medicine dances?"

"It is good," nodded Looks Far.

They talked more as they rode on, for which Wolf's Head was glad. Perhaps Looks Far was now distracted from his personal problem, whatever it might be.

They discussed the condition of the prairie, the growth of the grass. It was good this year. This would mean the return of many buffalo for the fall hunt.

If, of course, there were a fall hunt. That ominous thought was left unsaid, but both medicine men were only too aware of it. By the time the buffalo returned, there might be only Blue Paints on the prairie to do the hunting.

They stopped their travel early that evening, and picketed the horses in a grassy meadow. Both men carried the equipment of their profession as they climbed the hill to watch the sunset and prepare their ceremonies.

There must be a fire, and Looks Far drew out his fire sticks. In only a little while, a small, compact blaze was ready. The two men drew out their materials and painted their faces for the dance.

In all of the thousands of seasons of human hunters on the prairie, this may have been the first time that medicine men of enemy tribes assisted each other in their ceremonies. Certainly it was the first for these two.

Sun Boy's colors were radiant tonight. His choices included brighter and more spectacular hues of orange, pink, and purple than either of the men had ever seen. Both thought it a good sign.

Wolf's Head danced first, while Looks Far assisted by keeping cadence on a small dance drum. Wolf's Head adjusted the wolfskin headdress and cape and tied the thongs under his chin.

"How is your beat? Like this?"

"Yes, a little slower at first—so—"

"Ah, yes, much like ours."

Looks Far could not understand the words of Wolf's Head's song, but the effect was much like that of his own. The staccato sounds of the turtle-shell rattles on the medicine man's ankles, the gourd noisemakers in his hands, and the rhythmic drumbeat seemed to blend with the song, ascending to the darkening sky.

Occasionally Wolf's Head paused to take from his pouch a pinch of some powdered plant material. This he would toss on the fire, producing a sudden flare of light and a puff of sweetly aromatic smoke. Looks Far marveled that the ritual was so nearly like his own. He could even identify the source of the aromatic incense by the smell of the smoke.

He was certain that the song was much the same, also. There would be thanks to Sun Boy, or Sun, for causing the grass to grow, and pleas to continue. There were prayers for timely return of the buffalo, and for success in the hunt.

The present situation called for further pleas. There must be prayers for success in the coming battle, and help in driving the invaders from the Sacred Hills. Looks Far watched the sweat bead the brow of Wolf's Head and run down his face, streaking the ceremonial paint on his cheeks. Faster and faster the rhythm of the dance moved, until at last he fell to his knees, facing the sun's last rays.

Now it was time for Looks Far to dance. Standing to full height, he raised the ceremonial whistle, made of an eagle's wing bone, and blew the announcement of the ritual. He saluted the four directions, and then again the retreating Sun Boy.

Aside from the symbolic accoutrements of the rituals, his dance and song were much like that of the other. At one point in the ceremony, he paused to draw out the elk-dog medicine, the Spanish bit, placing the thong around his neck with solemn dignity. This part of the ritual had been improvised in the last few generations, since the coming of the horse. Other parts had been with the People since First Man came through the log.

Sun Boy had retired to the Other Side and the moon was setting by the time the dance was finished.

"It is good," stated Wolf's Head unequivocally, almost reverently.

Both men were deeply moved by the ceremonies, their own as well as each other's. There was a closeness between them, now. They had participated in each other's medicine, and both felt a warm, spiritual calm.

It was unnecessary to talk. They extinguished the fire, repacked their medicine bags, and sought their robes. It was a long time, however, before sleep came to either. There was a sense of awe, somehow, a supernatural quality about the night. Tired though they were, it seemed inappropriate to sleep, for they might miss the greatest experience of a lifetime. Both felt, they later agreed, that this night they had come very close to understanding the spirit of the Sacred Hills.

30

》 》 》

Looks Far wakened to find that it was nearly day. He lay for a moment, trying to remember where he was, and the circumstances. It had been long since he slept so well.

Turning his head slightly, he could see the muffled figure of his companion rolled in his robe against the chill of the prairie night. Ah, yes, Wolf's Head. Events of the past few moons rushed back at him, causing Looks Far to spring to a crouching position, alert for danger.

A horse called from below, and he realized that this had been the sound that had wakened him. Quickly he rose to survey the distant prairie. The horse might be calling to others of its kind, perhaps wild horses. It might only be inquiring, "Is any horse out there?" On the other hand, the animal might sense the approach of horses ridden by enemies. Looks Far had always marveled at the great distances over which a horse can sense the presence of another.

He had asked his father about it. Horse Seeker, it was said, knew more about the inside of an elk-dog's head than anyone in the tribe. It had once been a matter of life and death for him to think like the wild horses.

"I do not know, my son," Horse Seeker had answered the question with a thoughtful smile. "I am made to think that their spirit reaches out farther than ours, and that other elk-dogs feel it at greater distance."

He had paused a moment for a long breath.

"I have wondered," he mused, "if we could learn to reach out with our spirits, like the elk-dog."

Now the thoughts of Looks Far were brought back to the present by his companion. Wolf's Head was sleepily rolling from his robes.

"What is it, Looks Far?"

"I do not know. The horses called."

Both men stepped to the highest point of the hilltop, straining to catch any glimpse of something out of the ordinary. Sun's rim was barely showing above the edge of the world. The medicine men instinctively looked to the north, where the Blue Paints were expected to be. It was well that their attention was not entirely in that direction.

"*Aiee!*" exclaimed Wolf's Head, pointing. "There!"

To the west, far in the distance, there appeared to be movement on the prairie. At first it was difficult to distinguish from the scattered bands of elk, antelope, and buffalo. The movement did not appear random, but a steady motion of a number of creatures from north to south. Ah, thought Looks Far, to have eyes like the eagle! Then they could easily see.

"We must go and look," stated Wolf's Head.

"Yes."

They snatched their robes and medicine bags and turned down the hill to the horses. Looks Far quickly swung the grass-filled saddle pad to his mount's back and tied the thongs that held the medicine bag. It took only another moment to loop the medicine knot around the animal's lower jaw. He vaulted onto the saddle, turning to look for Wolf's Head.

"Careful!" the other man signaled, using hand signs.

Looks Far nodded, and the two reined the horses around to head up and out of the little meadow. Their course now became extremely important. They must reach a point high enough to see what was occurring on the prairie, yet remain concealed from searching eyes. Wolf's Head pointed to a ravine that led in the general direction they sought, and which offered some concealment.

They threaded their way among brush and small trees, climbing slightly as they progressed. Nearing the head of the gully, the riders paused.

"Is there a way out?"

"Who knows? We could go back."

"No, there is a game trail."

Looks Far pointed to the dim path they had been following. True, such a trail might lead only to a spring at the head of the little canyon. Their position was becoming dangerous. If enemies entered behind them, and there was no way out, *aiee*, it would be bad medicine.

There was, indeed, a spring, nestled among the rocks. The two dismounted to drink. It might be long before another chance offered. While the horses drank, Wolf's Head poked around among the rocks. Looks Far remained with the animals to prevent too much drinking of water. A horse with an overfull belly would be slow and heavy.

"Here," motioned the Head Splitter. "A trail."

It was hardly a trail. A spot here and there among the jumbled stones above the spring, where no grasses grew. It was easy to see why. These were the only spots where there was footing secure enough to provide a place to step. Deer, antelope, and other animals had used this exit on occasion.

The two men remounted and turned the horses toward the rocky slope. Reins slack, leaning forward upon the withers, they allowed the animals to choose the path. They would instinctively choose the easiest trail.

Slowly, halting for a moment, then scrambling ahead, they climbed. Sun was well up when they emerged near the crest of the ridge into the open again. Both men breathed a sigh of relief. They were people of the open prairie, who felt trapped in an enclosed setting, where the far horizons could not be seen.

Just now, however, they approached the open crest

cautiously. They tied the horses to a scrubby tree below the rim, and crawled to the crest.

It was a moment before they were able to reorient themselves and look for the moving creatures. Then both pointed at once.

"Aiee!"

It was Looks Far who voiced the whispered exclamation. Across a distant hilltop to the west filed a number of mounted warriors. There were at least thirty already in view, and more were coming in sight even as they watched. Not again would the Blue Paints underestimate their enemy. Any war party now scouting the plains would be in strength.

"They still come!" exclaimed Wolf's Head. "How many?"

"At least forty, now. Wolf, they are heading toward Sycamore River."

"Yes, but our warriors will scatter. That is the plan."

They must depend on the skills of their own warriors to elude the enemy war party. There was nothing that the two could do now to warn them. It would be best to remain in this concealed position until the Blue Paints were gone.

They assumed more comfortable positions and settled down to wait, casting occasional glances at the enemy party. It was frustrating to do nothing, and Looks Far resorted to one of the pastimes he had found amusing as well as useful. He began to watch the small creatures that peopled the rocky hillside.

A green lizard scuttled to the top of a nearby rock and sat sunning himself, meanwhile staring at the intruders. The shadow of a circling hawk flitted across the hill and the lizard vanished into a hole under the rock.

A tiny bird began to scold, and Looks Far noticed a fat, blue-black snake flowing smoothly along the ground beneath it. It took only a moment to locate the nest with fledglings in a bush near the scolding bird. Now the creature fluttered as if wounded, striking the ground near the snake and crippling away, with plaintive cries. Instantly the snake was alert, stalking, ready to strike.

But the bird fluttered a little way and paused. Again the snake moved, almost within striking distance, but the apparently crippled bird escaped once again.

Looks Far smiled. It was an old game. He felt a sense of satisfaction when the bird finally made what seemed an instant recovery and flew away. The dull-witted snake lay there a little while, and then slithered on down the hillside, away from the forgotten nest with its two fledglings. The mother bird had deceived her enemies once more, and saved her brood.

A quick flash of motion caught his attention and he turned his head. It was only a rat, the shy scampering creature seldom seen except at night. His glance now fell on the animal's lodge—a huge mass of dry sticks and trash stuffed under a bush and between the rocks. He had always marveled at how, and why, the small creature built such a dwelling, larger than two men could encircle with their arms. Such a dwelling was useful, of course, to the People. The dry twigs from a pack rat's nest were ideal for starting a camp fire.

Slowly an idea began to form.

"Wolf's Head!" he cried. "We can confuse the Blue Paints, and cause them delay."

He pointed to the rat's nest.

"We can burn it!"

Wolf's Head started to argue, but then began to understand. An unexplained smoke on the plains would need investigation by the Blue Paints' war party. It would require some time to be certain that no band of warriors lurked in the hidden canyon.

"We must be ready to ride."

"Yes. Get the horses ready while I make the fire."

Looks Far took out his fire sticks and gathered a tuft of dry grass. He approached the nest with all the formality of a visit to the lodge of a friend.

"Little brother," he spoke softly, "we must use your lodge. You can build another."

Small flames were licking around the base of the rocky crevice before the rat jumped out and scurried to safety. By this time, the horsemen were mounted and traveling rapidly away from the area.

Looks Far chuckled to himself as they rode. He could imagine the enemy war party, spending the entire day carefully stalking a smudge of greasy smoke that proved nothing but a rat's nest.

31
» » »

Twice more, before they joined the rest of the war party, the medicine men paused to set fires. It was easy to imagine the consternation of the enemy when they saw widely separated spirals of smoke on the prairie. They would have no choice but to investigate each one, causing delay in their movements.

The two talked that evening of the possibility of each warrior firing a rat's lodge here and there as he traveled. There was danger, of course, that too many such incidents would cause the Blue Paints to ignore them altogether. Still it was a possible tool. Any delay in the advance of the invaders would be useful, as the combined tribes gathered fighting men for the coming war. The greatest danger was to be forced into combat too soon.

Again, Looks Far wondered desperately, what if after all, with the fighting men of both tribes assembled, they did not have enough strength to halt the invasion? What if, farther to the north, there were even more Blue Paints, and more and more beyond that, coming and coming until they overran the plains? It was not a pleasant thought, but might easily be an accurate one. The Blue Paints showed no inclination to pause in their invasion, even after recent losses.

If there were only some way, some powerful medicine that would help the People and their allies. If they could draw the spiritual strength of the Sacred Hills and use it for their own.

The two medicine men spoke long about it that night. Both feared the same thing, that even their combined strength could not match that of the Blue Paints.

"Wolf's head," his companion inquired, "tell me of your other bands. Will they come to help?"

"Who knows? You must understand these people, my friend. They are independent, headstrong, and do not like to be told what to do. You know that we do not even have a Sun Dance, like yours?"

"You have no Big Council of all bands, no Real-chief?"

"Sometimes. Mostly, one of the band chiefs has enough influence to call the others to council. If he does not, they do not come."

"So they will come if they respect Lame Bear's request?"

"Yes, but it is more than that. They will decide if it seems more important than other things, like the fall hunt. It depends much on what sort of year they have had. But if they decide to come, they will be able fighters."

"Yes, I know. My people have feared them for many and many seasons."

"My fear," said Wolf's Head slowly, "is that even if they come, and even if they are here soon enough, we will not have enough strength. My brother, these Blue Paints are mighty."

"Yes," nodded Looks Far. "How soon will we know if your other bands come?"

"Maybe a moon. Do you think that is too late?"

"Who knows? We need strong medicine, my friend. You and I must find it."

Looks Far refrained from telling the other man how depressed he had found the Real-chief. He had thought much about that. There was something missing. There was no leader to follow. Yellow Hawk could have been a uniting force, a chief to inspire confidence and strength. The combined force could have followed him, but not with his present doubts. His indecisiveness would spread, making the entire fighting force ineffective.

And what other leader was there? Standing Bird was old, the other band chiefs not strong enough in leadership ability. The People would never follow Lame Bear, their recent enemy.

Once more Looks Far returned to the same point. Some great revelation was necessary, some powerful medicine, to accomplish their goal. The goal: survival for the two tribes.

They reached Sycamore River, and were met by a warrior who led them to the hidden camp. Looks Far was pleased to see that the war party seemed relaxed and confident. At least these men could be counted on to oppose the invaders. Lodge Pole greeted them with a smile.

"*Ah-koh*, my brothers. You have seen the Blue Paints?"

"Yes, but we were not seen. We set fires to confuse them."

"*Aiee!* We saw smoke!" Lodge Pole laughed in delight.

"You have seen Blue Paints?"

"Only at a distance. There are many, Looks Far! We have kept hidden. How is it at the main camp?"

Looks Far waited long before answering. What could be said?

"More of Wolf's Head's people may join us, but Yellow Hawk's heart is unsure of the battle."

"*Aiee*, it is not good! He must have the strength of eagles!"

Looks Far nodded. How could he tell Lodge Pole that there seemed to be no leader, no war chief who could organize the defense? He suspected that Lodge Pole knew.

"Wolf's Head and I search for powerful medicine to meet the Blue Paints."

Somehow, when put into words, the possibility sounded hopeless.

Lodge Pole walked beside him as he picketed his horse with the others. The tall man seemed to be waiting for something. Finally he broke the silence.

"You have talked to Blue Dawn?"

How stupid of me, thought Looks Far. Of course, he wants to hear of her. The thought crossed his mind that he had forgotten on purpose, because of the uncomfortable feeling that he now had each time he thought of the girl.

"Oh, yes, forgive me. Of course I talked to your wife. She sends—"

He broke off in mid-sentence at the astonished look on the long face of Lodge Pole. The young man's jaw had dropped open, his eyes widened, and he looked as if his spirit had suddenly escaped his body.

"*Aiee*, Looks Far," he finally muttered. "I have no wife. There is one in my own band to whose father I will someday speak, but—"

Now Looks Far was confused and irritated.

"Lodge Pole," he snapped, "do you think me a fool? You lived in her parents' lodge!"

The lanky warrior took a deep breath.

"My friend," he began slowly, "you are mistaken. I was the guest of Lame Bear after the Blue Paints came. I slept in his lodge because it rained. The girl, my friend, is like a sister to me. She sees only you. That is why I asked you to talk to her."

A mixture of emotions rushed in on Looks Far. Regret, that he had missed the opportunity. Joy, that the girl felt affection for him. Despair, that with the hazards of the next few days, he might be killed before he could tell Blue Dawn of his feelings.

"My heart is heavy for you, my brother," Lodge Pole was saying sympathetically.

Anger rushed up into his throat like the taste of ashes. He nearly struck out at the solemn face of his friend, but then relaxed. It was not the fault of Lodge Pole.

"It is no matter, Lodge Pole. I will talk to her later."

To himself, he added another thought: if we are still alive.

32

» » »

His thoughts were often on the girl in the next few days. Even the slight possibility that she might accept his advances was a thrill of excitement. He tried to plan ahead, to think when and under what circumstances he might see her.

The frustration of it all was that he could see no way. With the expected conflict nearer by each day, he could not leave now on a personal mission. It would be inconsiderate of the others, as well as dangerous to himself and his people.

So his waking thoughts, when not occupied with more pressing matters, were of Blue Dawn. He would find a moment to think his own thoughts, and smile to himself. It was a strange mixed feeling, warm and quiet, yet thrilling and exciting. It made him want to run to the hilltop and shout to the sky of his affection for her.

His nights were filled with dreams of her. They were no longer troubled dreams, but quiet, comfortable visions. He would see himself, from an observer's view, as he walked hand in hand with Blue Dawn. Her long shapely body moved with all the grace of a willow in the wind, her stride matching his own as they walked. He saw her turn her face to look at his, pure adoration in her deep eyes. His countenance was no less adoring. She came into his arms.

Then he would wake suddenly, embarrassed, irri-

tated at himself. He was behaving like the most inexperienced novice warrior, fresh from the Rabbit Society
of childhood.

He sought out Lodge Pole. He must talk to someone
about the girl, to ask of her likes and dislikes. It
seemed strange to him that he really knew so little of
her, was actually only slightly acquainted. How could
it be that he held her in such high regard, that he felt
affection, even love, for a virtual stranger? He could
not ask such things of Lodge Pole, but could talk of
her. That might help the yearning in his heart.

"Lodge Pole, tell me of the girl, Blue Dawn."

The lanky youth shrugged amiably.

"I do not know, Looks Far. What is there to say?
She has the heart of the eagle. She saved us all, and
maybe her tribe and ours."

"But, you and she, you are not—"

Lodge Pole smiled patiently again.

"No, my friend. It is as I told you. A storm was
coming, and Lame Bear invited me to shelter in his
lodge. The girl is like a sister. In fact," he paused, "she
reminds me much of my own sister."

"How so, Lodge Pole?"

"She is quiet and kind, but brave. She has respect
for her father."

"Lame Bear has two wives, besides the mother of
Blue Dawn?"

"Yes, and several children. But I think this girl
reminds him of her mother. She was his favorite, his
sit-by wife, I think."

Looks Far nodded. He would have been surprised at
the accuracy of this guess.

"Do the other wives treat her well?"

"Yes. They must, of course. But they like her. She
works hard and does not complain. I think that, too, is
like her mother."

Looks Far would have liked to pursue the subject of
the girl's interest in him, and how Lodge Pole knew of
it, but his dignity would not permit it. Instead, he
changed the subject.

"You spoke of a woman of the Mountain band, Lodge Pole. Do I know her?"

"I do not know. She is one I knew since a child in the Rabbit Society. Her name is Antelope Woman."

"You have spoken to her?"

"Not really. We talked as children, how we would have our lodge someday. But you know, that is only the talk of children."

"But important talk, my friend. You have not talked since you are grown?"

"Oh, yes, but not of that. We are friends, and have always felt that someday—you must remember, Looks Far, I have no horses, no lodge."

"Of course. These things come in their turn. But, Lodge Pole, you have a share in the captured horses."

It was difficult to realize that this young man was so young, he had shown such leadership. It would not be many seasons, Looks Far felt, before he became a respected subchief of the Mountain band. And when the time came for old Black Beaver to be replaced, the Mountain band could certainly do no better than this rising young warrior. He hoped that the childhood romance of Lodge Pole with young Antelope Woman would ripen into maturity, as well.

The scouts reported constantly on the movements of the Blue Paints. They seemed to be everywhere, and traveled in large parties. It was apparent that they were probing south in great strength. Since the war party had moved camp to Sycamore River, no group of Blue Paints had been seen that numbered fewer than forty warriors.

One scout, caught between two parties of the enemy, had released his horse and concealed himself in a tiny pocket in the rocks after hiding his saddle. The Blue Paints had seen the animal and shown only mild interest, apparently believing it to be a wild horse. There were many on the prairie, and this was what the scout had hoped. He waited until darkness, and traveled on foot to rejoin the others. He was one of the Head Splitters, and it was said afterward that the terror of his escape through the darkness had turned his hair white, overnight.

Still another young man, a quiet youth from the Red Rocks band, went out on a scout to the north and simply disappeared. When he did not return, two others went to search, though possibly only for his body. They found no trace, and White Dog was never seen again.

This cast a cloud over the entire group. To die honorably in combat was of no consequence, but simply to disappear? This led to a rumor that the Blue Paints were somehow supernatural, that their medicine was so powerful that they could destroy even the spirits of their enemies, and make it as if they had never been.

The concerned medicine men called the warriors together. Looks Far spoke first, Wolf's Head translating for the Head Splitters.

"My brothers, I hear it whispered that the Blue Paints have strong medicine."

There was no sound, only the quiet rattle of cottonwood leaves overhead.

"Now consider, all of you. How many of them have we killed? Thirty? Forty? And how many have we lost? Only a few! Does this seem like powerful medicine to you?"

He paused to let the thought penetrate for a moment.

"But, Looks Far," one of the young men protested, "there are more of the Blue Paints now than before."

"But they are only flesh and bone," broke in Wolf's Head, "no different than we are."

"Flesh and bone, yes. But maybe they are like the shiny lizard who lives under rocks. When he is caught, he breaks in pieces, escapes, and lives again!"

It was hard to argue with such logic. Wolf's Head paused and glanced to Looks Far for support. Then another warrior in the circle spoke, almost unheard, but devastating in the impact of his question.

"And where is White Dog?"

Looks Far was almost desperate now. This problem he had not foreseen. The most loyal, dependable warriors of both tribes, chosen for this special mission, were wavering. The insecurity of facing the unknown was threatening to destroy their effectiveness.

"Look, my brothers," Wolf's Head almost shouted, "do not fear the Blue Paints' medicine. Looks Far and I have stronger combined medicine than any they can use. We wait only until there are enough of them in one place."

"There are many now, Wolf's Head! It is time to use your medicine!"

"Our medicine has worked!" insisted Wolf's Head. "We have killed twenty to their one!"

The opinion of the group still wavered, though the argument of Wolf's Head was a valid one.

"Looks Far and I have an even more powerful plan, which you will hear later."

Indecision still hung in the air, but now a sentry who had been posted slipped quietly back to the group.

"My brothers," he called quietly, "someone comes."

Everyone quieted and hurried to concealment. A lone rider descended the slope at a walk, holding his right hand aloft in the universal peace sign. His facial paint and the manner in which his hair was braided identified him as a Blue Paint. Eager hands fitted arrows to bowstrings.

But the rider stopped, just out of bowshot. Hand still raised, he called out to the unseen warriors.

"Looks Far? Wolf's Head? It is Red Feather!"

33

Red Feather told his story as he scrubbed away the blue facial paint and rebraided his hair. He had reached the Eastern band without difficulty, and made an impassioned plea for help. Even so, he was able to recruit only a dozen warriors.

They had started back, and had soon encountered large numbers of Blue Paints. They managed to evade the enemy, but most of the warriors of the Eastern band had decided that the enemy was too powerful to oppose. All but two men defected and started home. Red Feather did not know what had happened to them, but was appropriately bitter. It was plain that he no longer felt any allegiance to the Eastern band.

Meanwhile, he and two others had pushed on. They had had misfortune in choosing a hiding place. They were hiding by day and traveling by night, and had stopped at dawn one morning, in a densely wooded draw. A war party of Blue Paints had arrived later, before dark, and had begun to set up a camp. It was apparent that they expected to stay the night, perhaps longer. The three men of the People separated to lose themselves in the rocks and underbrush.

One had been captured and killed, Red Feather knew. He had heard the shouts and screams. The prisoner had died slowly. He was not certain of the other. Near dark he had released their horses to mingle with those of the enemy.

His escape had been a mixture of good luck and ingenuity. As he lay hidden, a lone warrior had almost stumbled over him. The man was carrying an armful of sticks for the campfire, and hurriedly dropped them to attack. Both men were equally startled, but Red Feather, with strength born of desperation, managed to strangle his assailant.

He lay panting from the exertion for a moment, expecting others to rush in, but there was nothing. An idea began to form as he studied the still body beside him. They were in a tiny hidden clearing among the willows, and his attacker had merely blundered in, searching for firewood.

Red Feather noticed a medicine pouch at the man's waist, and realized that it might contain articles of use to him. Quickly he drew forth the blue-white paint, and adorned his own face, copying the patterns from the face of the dead warrior.

Next, he untied his hair, rough-combing with his fingers, and rebraided it in the style of the enemy.

Lastly, he stripped the hunting shirt of unfamiliar design from the warrior who had no further use for it, and slipped it over his own. In the gathering dusk, he was able to move among the enemy without being detected.

He had decided, if he were stopped, to use sign talk. He would declare that he was from another band of the Blue Paint people, and had taken a vow of silence until the new country was secure. As a last resort, he was prepared to fight to the death, rather than face capture and torture.

As it happened, neither course was necessary. He had not been challenged, and had been able to steal a horse and make his way south. He had allowed the paint to remain on his face, and the rest of his disguise intact, in case he encountered other parties of Blue Paints.

"Now," Wolf's Head demanded of the surrounding warriors, "whose medicine is more powerful?"

This was difficult to deny. Looks Far saw a sense of confidence, of optimism, in the party. The return of

Red Feather provided a badly needed impetus for these warriors.

One of their problems, he knew, was that they had been unable to strike in the prearranged manner. There were simply too many Blue Paints on the prairie. The strike and run tactics had been badly inhibited by the sheer overwhelming numbers of the enemy. There was no place to hide after each strike. Even their present camp on Sycamore River would be in danger at any time.

After Red Feather had rebraided his hair and removed the enemy shirt, the medicine men drew him aside. In the excitement of Red Feather's personal triumph, Looks Far had not overlooked the fact that he had gone for help and returned with none. Not only that, the story of Red Feather reinforced their impression that the plains were teeming with the invading Blue Paints.

Red Feather agreed.

"They are as many as leaves in autumn, my friends," he spoke solemnly. "You have sent word to our people?"

"Yes, about our war party's first successes. None since then."

"Not about the Blue Paints' move?"

"Their move? What is this, Red Feather?"

"*Aiee!* You did not know? They have struck their lodges, and their entire nation is moving. They come this way. They will be here in three, maybe four sleeps!"

Wolf's Head and Looks Far stared at each other in amazement. Yes, this must explain the increasing strength of the enemy war parties. The entire Blue Paint nation was on the move, deeper into the Sacred Hills. Their own scouts, probing only a limited radius, had encountered only scouting patrols of the Blue Paints, rather than the main column.

"We must tell our people at once," Wolf's Head spoke. "The war comes sooner than we thought."

"Yes. Your other bands will come too late, my friend."

"Yes. Looks Far, do you have a plan?"

Looks Far shook his head. Now the hopelessness of the entire situation settled like a dead weight on his shoulders.

"I do not know. Their scouts probably already know where our main camp is. They can camp nearby and raid whenever they like, until we are all dead."

"Then we must attack them while they are still moving, before they choose a camp."

Red Feather and Looks Far agreed.

"Let us choose the spot. We can send word to the main camp, where the battle must be."

"Yes," agreed Wolf's Head, "and it must be near Sycamore River. The Blue Paints will be here in three sleeps, and our warriors can be here first. This is as good a spot as any."

It was decided. One man would carry the message, while the rest of the party waited for the approach of the enemy. Scouts would move out farther, attempting to locate the main Blue Paint column, and reporting back to the camp at Sycamore River.

Looks Far suggested that the messenger be Lodge Pole. He would have preferred to go, himself, but felt that his responsibility lay here. Lodge Pole was known to both tribes, and his message would be respected. Besides, the young man deserved an opportunity to see his intended wife.

"My brother," Looks Far spoke to him privately, "will you speak to Blue Dawn for me? Tell her," he paused in embarrassment, "that I misunderstood. Tell her I would speak with her when we meet again."

The long face of Lodge Pole split in a broad grin.

"Of course, Looks Far. And next time, you speak for yourself."

He hurried away, riding hard to the south.

Looks Far sat, dejected. There were too many things wrong. There would probably be no next time, for him to speak with Blue Dawn. His mission at best was one of suicide. At worst, the Blue Paints could simply bypass the armed force at Sycamore River, and attack the undefended camp of the People. It might be, even, that Lodge Pole would be unable to reach the tribe with his urgent message. This would place only the small strike party to meet the horde of invaders.

Red Feather sought a borrowed robe to catch some much-needed sleep. As he passed the seated medicine men, he paused for a moment.

"It is too bad," he commented offhandedly, "that the fall hunt is spoiled. The buffalo come early, and in great numbers. They are only one or two sleeps north of the Blue Paints."

He moved on without waiting for comment. It was an indication that he understood the gravity of the situation. The fall migration of the great herds was the lifeblood of the People. Now there appeared an exceptional opportunity for a great harvest, but it could not be. Even if the People survived the war with the invaders, they would be unable to take advantage of the opportunity to hunt. They would go into the winter months with few supplies, facing starvation.

Looks Far felt that his world was falling to pieces under him. If anyone had a fall buffalo hunt, it appeared, it would be the Blue Paints.

34

>> >> >>

Looks Far slept little. There were too many thoughts on his mind. For a long time he watched the Seven Hunters circle the Real-star. His mind kept returning to the buffalo, and the impossibility of the hunt. Surely something could be done. It was not until after the half-moon poked a tentative orange finger above earth's rim that his thoughts finally began to bear fruit. Then he could hardly restrain himself.

He tossed his robe aside and crept to one of the sleeping forms.

"Wolf's Head! Wake up! I must talk to you."

Without answer, the medicine man rolled from his bed. It appeared that he had not slept, either, so rapid was his response.

The two walked a little way in silence, and paused when they came to the edge of the thin strip of timber. The rolling prairie spread before them to the edge of the world, gray and silver in the pale light of the rising moon.

"You could not sleep either, Looks Far?"

"No. But hear me, my friend. I think I have found our medicine."

They sat on a fallen cottonwood and talked for some time, Looks Far describing his plan, the other man listening. Occasionally Wolf's Head interrupted with a question or comment. At last he spoke.

"Yes. It is good, Looks Far. This is the medicine we

need. But there is little time. The Blue Paints will be
at Medicine Rock before two sleeps."

Now both men were excited. Their scheme would
take much planning and much hard riding.

"It will have to be done before anyone can reach us
from the main camp. We must use only the warriors
we now have."

"Yes, Wolf's Head. We must leave now, and travel
hard before daylight."

They hurried to wake the others.

"Come. Our medicine is ready!"

"What is happening?"

"We will tell you as we travel."

Warriors whose survival depended on instant alert-
ness did not take long to awaken. By the time the last
began to roll from their robes, the first were tossing
saddles and equipment on their horses.

"We head for the Real-star," both medicine men
were passing the word. "We gather again before daylight, so stay close together. We will tell you of the
powerful medicine then."

"Looks Far, what if we are separated?"

"Then we meet at Medicine Rock. We must be
there before the Blue Paints."

They pushed the horses as fast as was safe, covering
much ground in the time before dawn. As the eastern
sky began to pale, Looks Far signaled the scattered
riders and pointed to a clump of trees on a hilltop
ahead. The riders drew together, and dismounted to
rest their horses and themselves, and to hear the words
of the medicine men.

"My brothers," Looks Far began, "this is the most
important medicine that any of us will ever make. It
depends on us all. Some of us, maybe all, may be
killed, but we can save our people."

He paused while Wolf's Head translated.

"Now, we are entering country where the Blue Paint
scouting parties are active. We will separate, to meet
again at Medicine Rock tonight. Now we will tell you
how the medicine will work."

He knelt to draw diagrams in the dust, now clearly seen
as dawn brightened. There were gasps and exclamations.

"*Aiee!*"

"It is good!"

"Looks Far, can you really do this?"

"Of course they can, stupid one!"

"But," interjected Wolf's Head, "it will work only if
everyone does his part."

The party separated to travel rapidly but carefully
through the day. The two medicine men rode together,
discussing the last details of the plan.

"Do you have everything you need?"

"Yes, except the calf skin. You use your wolf cape?"

"Yes. We must only select the place."

It was shortly before dark when they reached the
abandoned camp at Medicine Rock. The bodies of the
previously ambushed Blue Paints were gone, probably
carried off by their own people. Two men were already there, Head Splitters both, casting anxious glances
into the darkening woods. They had seen Blue Paints, but
only at a distance, they reported, and were undetected.

Red Feather rode in, reporting that he had seen no
one.

"Come, let us look for the proper spot," Looks Far
suggested. "Red Feather, come with us."

"We will return quickly," Wolf's Head assured his
warriors in their own tongue. "You wait for the others."

The three riders splashed across the river, and up
the steep path to the top of the bluff. A long, gentle
slope began at the rim, sloping up and back to the north
to blend into a ridge that ran parallel to the river, a
couple of bowshots away. Here and there the ridge
was broken at the crest by a jumble of rocks.

"There!" Wolf's Head pointed.

The three turned to inspect the clutter of huge square
stones, blocks broken from the buried limestone shelf
where it jutted from the slope.

"Yes, it is good. Now, where is Red Feather's place?"

They turned north again, mounting the ridge only
after carefully observing for any sign of the enemy.
From the vantage point of the ridge, they could see an

isolated hillock on the plain, with three small trees on its crest.

"There is my camp!" exclaimed Red Feather. "I will signal and then climb the tree."

"But, Red Feather," protested Looks Far, "if our plan does not work, you are helpless against the enemy."

"My brother," the quiet warrior answered, "if the plan does not work, it will not matter."

They sat a moment, studying the country beyond. In the lengthening shadows, they saw the movement at almost the same instant.

"Look! They come!" It was Wolf's Head who spoke.

In the distance, far beyond the trees chosen by Red Feather, range followed range of hills. The farthest were represented only by a bluish smudge against the sky. The nearer hills, however, would normally appear green. Tonight they were black, covered with the shifting and moving bodies of animals. The buffalo were coming.

"It is good," muttered Wolf's Head.

So far their plan was exactly on schedule.

35

» » »

After a quick council, and an explanation of the landmarks involved, the war party again scattered to move north. Wolf's Head and Red Feather remained at the river while Looks Far accompanied the others. They must quietly make their way into the buffalo herd.

They approached the scattered forefront of the herd, individual animals scouting ahead for better grass. These were old cows, the real leaders of the herd, though the bulls pretended to be so. Many of them had calves. This would make his task easier.

"Go on until you find good protection," he told the warriors. "I stop here. Good hunting!"

Now he must find a calf. It must be quiet and sure, so as not to excite the herd. A long time he waited, even after he had selected the right animal. Finally he was able to approach quietly, fitting an arrow as he moved.

"Little brother, I am in need of your shirt," he muttered apologetically as he drew the arrow to its head.

The calf jumped at the twang of the string and the hollow thunk of the arrow when it struck. It made no sound, and stood still, quietly lowering its head. Looks Far could imagine, even in the dim light, that he could see bloody froth forming at the nostrils of the dying calf. It was good, a lung shot. If the arrow had been misplaced, and had struck the heart, the animal might have run wildly until it collapsed, exciting the herd.

Now the mortally wounded calf lay down slowly, as if it were lying down for a brief rest. Cautiously Looks Far moved forward, drawing his knife. He quickly slit the skin up the belly, and stripped it from the carcass.

He tossed the skin over his shoulder and went to where his horse was tied. Now he could hurry back to the river, where Wolf's Head and Red Feather waited.

"I am ready." He held up the calf skin as he swung down from his horse. It would not be long until dawn.

"Here, I will help you," Wolf's Head offered. "Red Feather, take his horse.

"We left our horses in the woods at the bottom," he continued as he worked.

They spread the fresh calf skin over the head, shoulders, and back of Looks Far, arranging it carefully. Wolf's Head tied the skin around the arms and waist of the other. He was already wearing his ceremonial wolf robe.

"Here comes Red Feather. We go."

It was not yet full day when they started on foot up the slope. They passed the jumble of rocks they had seen before, and pointed it out to Red Feather once more.

"Here are my trees," observed that individual as they moved on up the slope.

He stepped aside.

"Be careful, Red Feather."

"Of course. Anyway, three is my medicine number."

He indicated the unmistakable reference, the three trees on the knoll.

Looks Far heaved a sigh. Much depended on this man, but he had proved himself worthy.

Now their only remaining decision was when to start their medicine. They could easily see the buffalo in the distance. They must wait until the Blue Paints approached, for everything depended on the proper moment.

The course of the river could be seen in both directions as it wandered across the prairie. Medicine Rock itself was not a rock at all, but a shelving bluff that rose along the stream for some distance. The People had always regarded the stark gray cliffs with some degree of awe. There had once been a belief that it was a place inhabited by evil, with dark, foreboding over-hangs and hidden caves.

In more recent generations, this was discounted. Now the People saw it as a very spiritual place, but one of neither good nor evil. It was merely a place with a powerful spirit of its own. Some even consid-ered that the spirits of the rock were helpful or harm-ful, depending solely on the intent of those who passed that way.

The two medicine men idly discussed these things as they waited, and the sun climbed in the sky.

"Your people think the Rock evil, Wolf's Head?"

"Some do. Bull's Tail, one of our greatest chiefs, was once defeated here by one man. But his life was spared."

Looks Far knew that story well.

"Yes, that was an uncle of mine, my grandfather's brother. Did you know that he lived alone in the Rock for a winter?"

"Our people were told that, but we did not believe it. Bull's Tail insisted to his dying day that there were others with him."

"I think not. Only the spirits of the place."

"I do not know. The entire war party of Bull's Tail was destroyed. There must have been strong medicine."

"Yes. My grandfather, Owl, always said so. He did not understand it, but he felt it."

"He was a medicine man, also?"

"Yes. He was the first to use both buffalo and elk-dog medicine."

Suddenly Wolf's Head sat up and looked to the northeast. Looks Far followed his pointing finger, and both concentrated their attention to that area.

In the far distance, a line of moving people wound its way over the ridge. The snakelike column became longer as it stretched across the plain. Soon the hid-den observers could see individual forms. Mounted warriors led the procession, women rode or walked beside pole-drags. Children and dogs were everywhere.

The travelers spread across the slope and approached the eastern end of the Medicine Rock bluffs. It would not be long until the head of the column came exactly in front of them. They crouched in their thin fringe of sumac, waiting. A glance behind showed the buffalo, still placidly grazing, coming closer.

Looks Far cast another look at the Blue Paint column. It now stretched from just in front of them to the hills in the northeast. More people were still streaming over the ridge in the far distance, now nearly obscured by the dust of their passing.

"Aiee," whispered Wolf's Head softly. "They still come!"

36
» » »

Whips-Along was relaxed that morning. It was a good day to travel, and the territory they would cross was easy and good.

This campaign was going well, and he was proud of his part in it. His Blue Paint people had discovered this choice area of lush, grassy hills, and had methodically moved to take possession. The current inhabitants had presented only minor problems.

True, there had been some ambush killings of small parties, but this had now ceased. Since the scouting parties had been increased in size, there had been no attacks.

He still chuckled at the grim joke they had played at the village they destroyed. That had been his idea, to display the heads on poles. It had struck terror to the inhabitants of these hills, and there had been little resistance since. Except, of course, for the ambush killings. The Grower tribes along the rivers were offering no resistance at all.

Now the scouts had located the big encampment to the south. It was the largest they had encountered, and apparently represented the main force of the tribes in the area. This would be the major battle as the Blue Paints assumed control of these tallgrass hills.

Whips-Along looked forward to the fight. He would count many honors. Although he was young, he had established a reputation already. Even his name said so.

That, he had acquired in a raid some years before. He had single-handedly captured an elderly Grower. The man professed to be a chief, but Whips-Along had disgraced him by making him walk in front of his horse. Each time the old man faltered, a quirt across the shoulders made him look alive again. The amused observers had commemorated the humor of the event by bestowing a new name on his captor.

Whips-Along looked forward to the capture of many horses in the coming battle. He thought of these things as he rode this morning. The big column, composed of the entire nation of Blue Paints, was guarded against surprise attack by flanking parties of riders. He was one of these.

Just now the task had become easier. The column was moving well, and was skirting along the river bluffs. The drop to the river effectively eliminated danger from that direction, so most of the flankers had moved to travel north of the column.

Now even that was unnecessary. Since daylight, the immense herd of buffalo that had been drifting into the area had moved farther south, and was grazing along the prairie, only a few bowshots away. Whips-Along knew that this was good. The presence of buffalo, grazing undisturbed, meant that no armed force of riders could approach from that direction. For most of this day's travel, then, the column was in complete safety.

It would be three or four sleeps before they encountered the warriors from the big encampment to the south. That might prove to be an interesting battle. If this tribe avoided a fight, however, the Blue Paints would establish their camp, and kill the present inhabitants a few at a time until they were no longer a problem.

Whips-Along turned his horse and rode up the slope

a little way to look at the buffalo. The presence of the great herd was another good omen. It was tempting to make a kill or two, but not practical. There would be no time for the women to care for the meat and skins while the tribe was traveling.

He rode up the hill and turned to look at the long column. It wound in both directions along the bluff's top as far as eye could see. It would be nearly dark, it appeared, before the last of the pole-drags reached the level area beyond, which had been selected for the night's camp.

He turned to watch the quietly grazing buffalo. He became amused at the antics of a calf near the edge of the herd. It would dart out and scamper in the open for a moment, then back to the protection of the larger animals.

Another flash of motion, well out from the herd, caught his attention. A large gray wolf had noticed the calf, and crouched, waiting. Whips-Along sat very still. The unfolding scene was only a couple of bowshots away, and if he moved, he might disturb the wolf's hunt. He cared nothing for that, of course, but it would be amusing to see the creature drag down the bawling calf.

Now the calf seemed to notice the crouching figure, and moved forward curiously. In the inexperience of babyhood, the calf seemed to regard this creature as someone to play with. The two pranced and circled, farther away from the herd. A cow lifted her head and called a low warning, then stepped forward in mild concern. Others became alert, and moved across the slope.

The wolf and the calf were now nearing a jumbled pile of rocks on the slope, and perhaps a dozen buffalo were trotting forward, ready to assist the youngster. Suddenly the wolf made a lunge and the calf bleated in terror. Buffalo came running, and Whips-Along chuckled in amusement. He wished that the others could see, but the slight ridge parallel to the river blocked the scene from view. He could see both the buffalo herd and the column, but the travelers could not.

Then a strange thing happened. Both the wolf and the buffalo calf rose on their hind legs, and were not animals at all, but men. They ran together to the pile of boulders and crouched in hiding. Whips-Along had not recovered from the shock and surprise when another motion caught his eye. A third man, who had been crouching behind a clump of trees higher up the slope, rose and waved a robe. He was apparently signaling someone on the distant hills.

Angry and frustrated, Whips-Along shouted at the other riders and kicked his horse toward the men in the rocks. Now a group of cows was milling around uncertainly, unsure where the calf and the threatening wolf had gone.

In the space of a few heartbeats, however, Whips-Along became aware of a sound. It was like distant thunder to the north. He stopped to look. All along the slopes of the next range, buffalo were moving excitedly. He could catch glimpses of men on the hilltops, waving robes, and now could distinguish war cries. In a moment the human sounds were drowned in the muffled thunder of a thousand hooves as the herd began to run.

Whips-Along drove his horse downslope, yelling an excited warning. Even as he did so, he saw the herd begin to move as a gigantic brown wave, washing down the slopes as far as eye could see.

He saw the leading animals pause in alarm at the sight of the moving column of people. The pause was only for a moment as the pushing horde behind came crowding, shoving, trampling anything in its way.

People screamed, tried to escape, but there was nowhere to run. The mass of shaggy creatures thrust against the column, unable to save themselves, even. Men began to shoot at the leading buffalo, but the next wave scrambled over the fallen in the mad stampede. Some people began to jump from the cliff, hoping that the risk of death in the river or on the rocks

below was less than that of the crushing buffalo herd.
Horses, people, pole-drags, and baggage began to spill
over the rim into the river below.

Whips-Along found himself and his terror-stricken
horse pushed along without control. He fought, screamed,
kicked, and tried to escape the crush, but it was to no
purpose. His last conscious thoughts were of falling,
turning in the air with hundreds of shaggy bodies, and
the rocky riverbed rushing up at him.

37

>> >> >>

Wolf's Head and Looks Far crouched in the tiny pocket among the rocks while the buffalo herd split and swirled around them. It was hard to fight off panic. Thick, choking dust filled the air, the lungs, the eyes, and gritted in the teeth.

Looks Far began to cough uncontrollably, and could dimly see his friend also racked with coughing. He could not hear because of the thunder that continued to shake the earth. For a moment he wondered if the mass of thundering buffalo would cause the collapse of the rock itself.

Another fear that occurred to him was that a luckless animal would stumble and fall on top of their little crevice. They might be buried alive beneath a mountain of buffalo carcasses. How strange, he thought, that only a day or two ago he had feared that there would be not enough meat for the winter to avoid starvation.

He had no way to gauge the effectiveness of their medicine against the Blue Paints, beyond the muffled shouts and screams that were soon drowned in the rumble of shaking earth.

Just as Looks Far began to think it would never end, the sound began to fade, and the shaking of the earth beneath them seemed to be lessening. It seemed to move toward the west, and become fainter as it moved.

He raised his head, but at first could see little beyond

the thick fog of dust. Slowly it began to thin, carried away by the gentle south breeze. He could see a few buffalo, confused and injured, stumbling around in consternation.

But the Blue Paints were gone, as if wiped from the earth. As far as they could see in the thinning haze, the rim of the bluff showed no sign of human life.

"*Aiee*," muttered Wolf's Head at his elbow. "Our medicine is strong!"

Looks Far turned to look at his friend. The face of the other was heavily caked with dust.

"You are wearing new face paint," Looks Far grinned.

"You, too."

Sweat had turned the whitish dust in the air to dirty brown mud on their faces. Only the whites of their eyes and the gleam of teeth as they smiled broke the dull color of the mask.

Red Feather came trotting down the slope, also caked with dirt.

"It happened!" He almost shouted in delight. "It was as you said."

His eyes were wide with wonder. From his perch in the tree, he had had a good view of the entire scene.

"*Aiee*, it was terrible for a little while. I thought my tree would break!"

The pushing and thrusting of the great beasts had shaken the tree so violently that he had nearly been thrown to the ground.

The three men started to look around as the dust thinned. The sun now began to show through the haze to the west, bloodred as it sank toward the earth's rim. The dust raised by the retreating buffalo still hung in clouds over the prairie in that direction, giving strange colors to the sunset.

The herd had apparently turned to the west, following the river's course, after the first few hundred went over the rim. Now they were only a massive moving blur in the far distance.

Someone shouted from up the slope, and one of the Head Splitter warriors trotted toward them. He was excited, exultant, talking and gesturing to Wolf's Head.

"He says only a few Blue Paints survived," translated the medicine man.

He pointed to the northeast. There, huddled against the hill, were a few dozen people. They had been bringing up the rear of the column, and had managed to retreat to safety when the stampede occurred. They stood numb, confused.

Somewhere below the cliff, a child was crying. Looks Far's emotions rushed in on him, all the events of the last few moons, and the fears of his own children in a time of massive destruction.

"I will find the child," he pointed.

"It is good," Wolf's Head nodded. "We will wait here for the others."

Looks Far found his way to the path down the cliff, and carefully descended, listening as he went. He could not hear the child now. He stopped at the river and waited.

The air was better here. The trickle of sparkling water over the shallows sounded as if there had been no earth-moving event. But up and down the stream, as far as he could see, were dead and dying buffalo. Some were piled, many carcasses deep, partly in the river. Some were among, or partly in, the trees, some even hanging grotesquely among broken branches. Here and there, the bodies of horses and of people were intermingled with those of the buffalo.

The child whimpered again, and Looks Far turned to a clump of willows. A woman crouched there, holding the child. She was pretty, and there was fear in her dark eyes. She shielded the child with one arm, and held up the other against the expected blow.

Looks Far felt pity for her. Carefully he addressed her in the sign language.

"I will not hurt you, mother."

She did not answer, only glared at him with fear and hate.

"Come. It is over. I will take you to your people."

He turned to the path, waiting and beckoning to the frightened young woman in the willows. She stood, carrying the child, and hesitantly followed.

At the top, he pointed to the huddled remains of her tribe in the distance. He addressed her in the sign talk again.

"Tell your people that we will not attack them again. Our medicine has spoken today. You must go back where you came from."

The woman nodded, fear still in her eyes.

"I will tell them."

Wolf's Head approached, having seen the sign talk.

"Tell them also," he added, "we will send any others we find to your camp."

She nodded again and fled to join her people.

The other warriors were gathering, laughing and exchanging stories of the stampede. Only one was slightly injured.

"There is much to do before dark," Wolf's Head spoke to the group. "Let us camp below the cliff, on the other side. And tonight, we eat fresh meat!"

This was a welcome prospect. For some time they had subsisted on dried rations. Two warriors moved to select a fat carcass to butcher while others selected a campsite and began to build fires.

"When do you think our people will come?" asked Wolf's Head.

"Who knows?" shrugged Looks Far. "Tomorrow, I hope. There is much meat and many skins to care for."

They had sent a messenger to tell the main camp of the change in plans. If he were persuasive enough, the People would arrive tomorrow.

For the present, they began to cook quantities of meat. While the cooking progressed, men moved up and down the stream for some distance, trying to evaluate the situation. A few Blue Paint survivors were found, brought to the cliff top, and started on their way to the cluster of their own people down the river.

The Blue Paints had started their own fires, which could be seen in the gathering darkness. The light faded, and the stars began to appear like more campfires in the sky.

Looks Far and Wolf's Head sat staring into their fire, or watching the other warriors relax comfortably around the camp. It was the first time in many moons that they had been free of danger.

"My friend," said Wolf's Head quietly, "it is over."

38

>> >> >>

The People arrived next morning, led by Lodge Pole and the other men of the strike group. They had brought an advance party to help in any conflict in case the plan of the medicine men had not worked. Now they would begin to butcher and skin the buffalo, preparing the carcasses for further processing when the rest of the camp arrived.

Through the morning, people trickled into the area by twos and threes, then handfuls, and finally in great numbers. They fell to work at the butchering immediately. With the weather this hot, they must work rapidly. In only a day or two the vast quantities of meat would be only rotting carrion.

People constructed drying frames of willow, and thin slices of meat were draped over the rods as quickly as they were cut. The skins were pegged flat on the ground to await the long process of conversion to robes, lodge covers, and garments.

Through all of the busy activities, the story of the great victory spread. The two medicine men were the heroes of the day. The men of the strike party told again and again how Looks Far and Wolf's Head had enticed the herd to the right place at the right moment. The power of their combined medicine had been awesome.

After a few repetitions of the story, it had grown until, in the minds of some, the medicine men had actually caused the buffalo to arrive early, at the proper time for the plan. Some even whispered that perhaps they had made the herd appear out of nowhere by the power of their spells and incantations.

Regardless, it was a time of feasting and celebration, as well as hard work. The air was filled with the odors of cooking meat. People worked, ate, laughed, rested, and began again.

The surviving Blue Paints in the distance were still being joined by straggling survivors. They appeared to be butchering a few animals for meat, since most of their supplies had been lost. It was easy for Looks Far to feel sympathy for these ragged remnants of a proud tribe. A proud, cruel, and merciless tribe, he was forced to remind himself. The margin of their own survival had been too narrow to waste sympathy on these who had tried to eliminate his people.

"Looks Far, the family of Lame Bear is here."

It was Lodge Pole, bringing the news of the arrival. He stood with a boyish grin, waiting.

"I will come when I can!"

Instantly Looks Far was sorry he had been so curt. He did not understand why, himself, except that this meeting with Blue Dawn had assumed such importance now.

He was interrupted by the arrival of his own family, and pointed out to his mother the partially butchered animals that he had selected and dragged into the open with his horse. The children helped carry willow sticks for drying frames.

When the first strips of meat were hung, the youngsters again were pressed into service to shoo away insects, birds, and stray dogs.

Eventually, of course, Looks Far summoned courage to go and talk to Blue Dawn. He had never felt so clumsy in talk.

Lame Bear greeted him enthusiastically, clasping the younger man by the shoulders in his tribal greeting.

"Your efforts have brought much good," the chief signed.

"Yes. The medicine of Wolf's Head and mine worked well together."

Blue Dawn crouched nearby, slicing strips of meat. She did not look up. *Aiee*, she was making this difficult, Looks Far thought.

"Dawn," he blurted finally. "I would talk with you."

Blushing, smiling awkwardly, she stood. He wondered how much of the misunderstanding Lodge Pole had explained to her. She was not helping him out of this embarrassing situation.

"I know you are busy now," he mumbled. "It is good to see you again. Can we talk later?"

"Of course. I am glad to see you, also. We can talk now, if you wish."

"I mean alone."

It made no difference that no one else within earshot could understand the language. He could not bring himself to talk to her under such circumstances.

"Later, then," she murmured.

She seemed confused, so he tried again.

"Did Lodge Pole tell you what I wished to say?"

"No, only that you wished to see me."

This was going very poorly.

"Dawn, I am sorry. I misunderstood. I saw Lodge Pole living in your father's lodge, and I thought . . ."

His voice trailed off. Now he had made himself appear completely demented. *Aiee*, how stupid.

But Blue Dawn was smiling at him. Now she seemed to understand, all at once.

"Looks Far," she smiled, "I will be pleased to see you. Come back this evening."

"Your father will not mind?"

"He will be pleased. You are a great man."

Looks Far felt like a great man as he made his way back to his family and the afternoon of hard work that waited.

39

>> >> >>

The two young people walked out onto the prairie. The shadows were long, and the cooling of evening had begun. There were fires, and the smells of cooking.

It would have been nicer, perhaps, for the couple to walk along the river, to listen to the talk of the water over white gravel in the shallows. Just now, however, the area along the river was a place of death and decay, so they sought the open grassland.

Somewhere the tentative thump of a drum told that a dance celebration was upcoming. It would be a time of rejoicing, of mingling of the two tribes, now allies, bound together by the events of the summer.

Looks Far was having a great deal of trouble initiating the conversation. Where should he begin? He had spent so long, thinking of this moment. Now that it had arrived, he was at a loss to begin. An owl called from the trees along the river, and a night bird sang his hollow, mysterious song. The chuckling cry of a hunting coyote seemed to come from very near. The creature and his tribe would eat well from the leavings at the river, they knew.

"The night is pleasant," the girl observed.

Looks Far nodded.

"Yes. It is a safe night. I wondered if we would see such a night again."

They walked, not speaking. Finally Looks Far approached the subject on both their minds.

"Dawn, I have thought much of you since you saved our lives."

"But I did nothing," she protested.

He held up a hand to silence her.

"No, you were important. Lame Bear might never have listened to us."

"It is over, now," she observed.

Also, she wished to add, the misunderstanding about Lodge Pole. She had been so puzzled about that. Looks Far had seemed quite interested in her, had appeared to return her affection for him, and then suddenly he had begun to ignore her. She had searched her memory for a hint as to what she might have done wrong.

Now she understood. The circumstances had been misleading, and Looks Far had been mistaken in his observations. Now they could begin again, but she could see that Looks Far was having difficulty. Maybe she could help him.

"You spoke of my father?"

It was a question, not a statement, an invitation to pursue the subject.

"Yes, I thought he might object to the interest of a man from outside your tribe."

"I think not, Looks Far. Anyway, we are allies now."

He nodded agreement. He was still finding this very clumsy.

"Dawn, would you object if I spoke to your father? I mean, to ask you to my lodge?"

He felt stupid, childish, to say the thought that was in his mind. To say it in words seemed so commonplace.

In the gathering twilight, the girl turned her face to him. It was as in his dream, her gentle smile, the adoring look in her eyes. She came into his arms, soft and yielding against him.

"I would be honored, my chief."

There was much to be done, many arrangements to make. Looks Far went to speak to Lame Bear that same evening. Blue Dawn had informed him of the proper approach, slightly different in custom from that of the People.

He must go and offer gifts to Lame Bear to compensate him for the loss of his daughter. She suggested perhaps six horses. Looks Far offered ten, and Lame Bear asked to see the horses.

The entire sequence seemed offensive to Looks Far. Among the People, traditions were different. Gifts were offered, but then the prospective son-in-law was welcomed into the girl's family. This negotiation seemed much like offering to buy the girl, and arguing over her worth. Well, he would do whatever was necessary.

Shortly after daylight, he drove ten of his finest horses to the Head Splitter camp and stopped before the lodge of the chief.

"My chief!" he called. "I bring your horses."

Lame Bear came outside, and casually looked over the animals. He examined each individual, lifting a hoof, checking teeth, stroking a glossy hide. Waiting, Looks Far grew irritated. This was hardly a horse trade.

Finally the chief straightened.

"It is good!" he proclaimed, smiling broadly.

Now came the time to arrange the ceremony. Blue Dawn wished to have the traditional ceremony of the People, with her father symbolically participating. In the end, Lame Bear agreed. He spread the robe around the shoulders of the couple to signify that they were now one.

Since Looks Far already had his own lodge, the newlyweds would move into it immediately. His parents were strong in their approval of this new daughter, who was after all, one of their own.

Several other romances blossomed in the ensuing days. The two tribes had spent enough time camped in adjacent areas for the young ones to find each other.

"It is good," smiled Yellow Hawk. "There is nothing better than marriage to strengthen an alliance."

The distant relatives of Blue Dawn, in the Red Rocks band, were pleased to welcome one of their own back to her own people. The girl had also endeared herself in other ways. She had gone to tell the mourning family of Broken Knife of the manner of his death, and of his bravery.

"He was a great chief," she assured them. "His was a big part in bringing the tribes together."

Her sympathy was well received, especially since Lodge Pole related that the girl had mourned for Broken Knife after the custom of the People.

Lodge Pole brought his intended wife to meet Looks Far and Dawn. She was a quiet, observant girl with a sparkling smile and quick wit.

"You have property, now," reminded Looks Far. "You can ask for her."

"Yes, I have spoken for her. We will be married soon."

They would live in the lodge of the girl's parents until their own lodge was finished. Lodge Pole saw this as an excellent opportunity for the acquisition of skins for a lodge, and was working hard and long to assemble them.

Red Feather, after much deliberation, decided to return to his Eastern band.

"It is good," Looks Far confided to Wolf's Head. "The Eastern band needs leadership."

They saw little of Wolf's Head, who was spending much time with his family after being away from them all summer.

40

There was no longer any need to remain at Medicine Rock. Every family had stored large quantities of dried meat and skins. Some of the older members of the tribe believed that never before had the People had so much food, so many skins as they entered the cold seasons. The few days they had spent at the Rock had been exhausting, with the hard work of salvaging meat, and the nights of dance and celebration.

Nights were cool with the hint of coming autumn, and the time had come to move to winter camp. The Red Rocks and the Mountain bands had far to travel to their traditional areas. The Northern band, still crippled from its losses, had elected to stay with the Southern band for the season.

Lame Bear's Head Splitters would return to their previous location. He had fervently assured the People of his lasting friendship, in open council. He promised to tell the other chiefs of his tribe of the events of the summer, and of the friendship and alliance of their two tribes.

Yellow Hawk, in turn, praised the role of the Head Splitters in the Great Medicine that had taken place. It would be retold in story and song forever. They exchanged gifts and vowed personal friendship. Yellow Hawk also extended a special invitation to the Head Splitters to join the People for the Sun Dance next season.

The alliance of the two tribes seemed firmly bound when a large party of warriors from other Head Splitter bands arrived. They had traveled fast and far to lend their help when the message arrived of a coming battle. It did not matter, now, that their help was not needed. They were welcomed as heroes, given food and lodging, and presented with gifts of appreciation.

But now it was time to move. The area along the river was becoming unpleasant because of the stench of rotting carcasses. They had salvaged hundreds, but there were hundreds more in the woods, among the rocks, and piled against the cliff. Even with the prevailing south breeze to drive the smells away from the camp, there was increasing unpleasantness. As the stream was increasingly polluted, it was necessary to go long distances for water.

In addition, it was hard to escape the ugly fact that this was a place of death. As they worked, they had encountered many bodies among the buffalo. With respect for the dead, these were carried and placed aside for the Blue Paints to come and care for.

It was puzzling that they did not do so. A delegation had gone to the Blue Paints to tell them that they might claim their dead, but they only nodded and stood numbly.

"I do not understand," Looks Far said to Wolf's Head, "a people who do not even care for their dead."

The other shook his head.

"Their medicine is strange. Maybe, though, they have no strength for it."

The two medicine men decided that this must be the answer. The few survivors simply could not physically care for the hundreds of bodies. So they remained, concerned more with sheer survival than anything else. The People continued to place the bodies aside as they were discovered. It was obvious that there might be many others beneath the mountains of rotting buffalo.

On the third day after the stampede, the remnant of the Blue Paint tribe had left the area.

"Look!" a lookout at the top of the cliff was pointing. "The Blue Paints are leaving!"

It was true. Those who climbed the bluff to watch saw the ragged little band make their way back on the trail they had followed so confidently three days before.

The scouts followed the Blue Paints for a few days. There seemed little doubt now. The invaders were leaving. Their might had been crushed, and it seemed unlikely that they would ever again have strength to be a threat to anyone.

Now, with cool crisp nights a reminder, Black Beaver announced that the move of the Mountain band would occur in two suns. The others quickly decided to follow suit.

It was always an exciting time when the tribe split up for the season. There was sadness because of leaving friends and relatives, yet anticipation of new places, new sights and sounds. The big lodges were coming down, lodge covers folded for travel, and poles sorted and tied or used for pole-drags.

Looks Far and Blue Dawn went to say their good-byes to her father. It was a scene filled with emotion. Looks Far addressed him in sign talk.

"I thank you for all your help, uncle," he used the sign of respect for adult males among the People. "Also for your daughter. I will care for her well."

"I know this," the chief signed in reply. "We will meet next year at your Sun Dance."

"It is good."

Looks Far stepped aside. His wife might wish a moment alone with her father. The girl sat on the ground beside him, unable to speak at first. Her eyes brimmed with tears.

"Father, I—There will be an empty place in my heart."

Gently, Lame Bear patted her head.

"I know."

There was something she wished to say, but was not quite certain what it was.

"Father, you know that I have always thought of myself as a woman of the Elk-dog People."

He smiled, a little sadly.

"Yes, your mother did that for you."

"You loved her very much."

He nodded, and now there was a tear in his eye, also.

"We have missed her, you and I."

Impulsively, she gave him a quick little hug.

"Father, I will always be proud to say that I am the daughter of Lame Bear."

"But, my child, you are not."

Blue Dawn's head whirled in confusion.

"Your mother never told you?"

"But, what—how?"

"My child, I could love you no more if you were my own, but your mother was already with child when she came to us. She did not come to my bed until after you were born."

"But who—" she struggled with this overwhelming news, trying to remember. Had her mother, ever at any time, given any indication?

"I always supposed that she had told you," Lame Bear was saying, "that this was why you thought yourself an outsider."

Suddenly she remembered, the long afternoons of stories about her mother's childhood, the wistful expression.

"Broken Knife!" she whispered to herself.

With a smile she hugged Lame Bear once more, and jumped to her feet.

"You will always be my father," she said happily, laughing through her tears.

She strode purposefully to her husband.

"Come," she smiled, "let us go."

"What is it, Dawn?"

"It is nothing, my husband. I will tell you later."

She took his hand, and they hurried to join the People.

Who Are "The People"?
» » »

Since the beginning of this series, a number of readers have asked which tribe "the People" represent. A Kiowa friend asks, "Are you writing about us?" A reviewer in Wyoming is confident they are the Northern Cheyennes. A Native American professor writes that the People "do seem much like (Southern) Cheyennes."

Actually the People are no particular tribe, but a composite. Since little is known of the sixteenth century in the Great Plains, it seems appropriate to describe a typical tribe of the buffalo culture, taking culture traits of several.

Most tribes referred to themselves as "the People" in their own tongues. For our tribe, I have used a modified Kiowa creation story, and deities and semi-deities common to several tribes. Their educational system, the Rabbit Society, is common to Kiowa, Arapaho, Comanche, and others.

Marriage customs are largely Cheyenne, and the Sun Dance is used in different forms by many tribes. The legendary Trickster is common to all plains tribes, by various names. The Gift Dance is Kiowa.

The culture of the People has grown with each book. Originally the Spanish contact was with the Southern band. This implies a Northern band. Bands to the west became the Red Rocks and the Mountain band. The Eastern band is known for foolish ways, a situation that occurs in several tribes. The camping arrangement at Big Council, and seating in the Coun-

cil itself, is assigned largely by geographic range. There
is, as in most tribes, an open space in the circle, facing
the rising sun, with heavy religious significance.

There has been mentioned another vacant spot in
the Council circle, once occupied by a sixth band, now
extinct. This situation appears in Kiowa culture.

Geographically the People range in a long oval,
bounded by the eastern slope of the Rockies, the eastern edge of Kansas, and from northern Oklahoma to
the Platte River. Of this region, the favorite camping
and hunting area of the Southern band is in the tallgrass
hills, the Sacred Hills of the People, the Kansas Flint
Hills of today.

Each tribe had enemies, and the traditional enemies
of the People are the "Head Splitters." Again, they
represent no specific tribe, merely "the enemy" as
seen by any tribe of such a culture.

The "Blue Paints" represent invaders of foreign culture. "Growers" could be any of a number of agricul-
tural tribes who lived along streams in the region,
while the "River People" to the northwest are a tribe
in the process of transition. Many farming groups,
when they acquired the horse, moved out onto the
plains to become hunters instead.

No doubt the People's culture will continue to ex-
pand, acquiring new customs with each new book
of the series. It is intended, however, that these char-
acteristics will be historically and sociologically accurate. That is, the People's complicated social structure
is authentic, representing various actual cultures of
the Plains.

If the reader feels that he recognizes the tribes described, that is good. It means that the writer is successful. He has made the People and their civilization
real, and their story will live.

DON COLDSMITH

1985

GENEALOGY

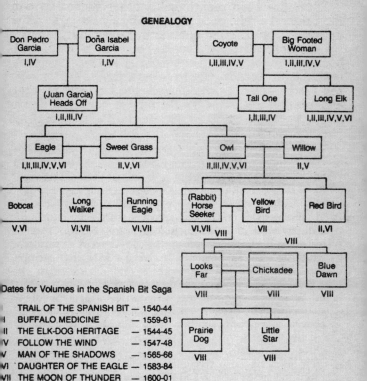

Don Pedro Garcia — I,IV	Doña Isabel Garcia — I,IV
Coyote — I,II,III,IV,V	Big Footed Woman — I,II,III,IV,V

(Juan Garcia) Heads Off — I,II,III,IV

Tall One — I,II,III,IV

Long Elk — I,II,III,IV,V,VI

Eagle — I,II,III,IV,V,VI

Sweet Grass — II,V,VI

Owl — II,III,IV,V,VI

Willow — II,V

Bobcat — V,VI

Long Walker — VI,VII

Running Eagle — VI,VII

(Rabbit) Horse Seeker — VI,VII VIII

Yellow Bird — VII

Red Bird — II,VI

VIII

Looks Far — VIII

Chickadee — VIII

Blue Dawn — VIII

Prairie Dog — VIII

Little Star — VIII

Dates for Volumes in the Spanish Bit Saga

I	TRAIL OF THE SPANISH BIT	— 1540-44
II	BUFFALO MEDICINE	— 1559-61
III	THE ELK-DOG HERITAGE	— 1544-45
IV	FOLLOW THE WIND	— 1547-48
V	MAN OF THE SHADOWS	— 1565-66
VI	DAUGHTER OF THE EAGLE	— 1583-84
VII	THE MOON OF THUNDER	— 1600-01
VIII	THE SACRED HILLS	— 1625-27

Dates are only approximate, since the People have no written calendar.
Volume II, BUFFALO MEDICINE, is out of chronological order, and should appear between Volumes IV and V.
Characters in the Genealogy appear in the volumes indicated.

ABOUT THE AUTHOR

DON COLDSMITH was born in Iola, Kansas, in 1926. He served as a World War II combat medic in the South Pacific and returned to his native state where he graduated from Baker University in 1949 and received his M.D. from the University of Kansas in 1958. He worked at several jobs before entering medical school: he was a YMCA group counselor, a gunsmith, a taxidermist, and, for a short time, a Congregational preacher. In addition to his private medical practice, Dr. Coldsmith is a staff physician at Emporia State University's Health Center, teaches in the English Department, and is active as a freelance writer, lecturer, and rancher. He and his wife of 26 years, Edna, have raised five daughters.

Dr. Coldsmith produced the first ten novels in "The Spanish Bit Saga" in a five-year period; he writes and revises the stories first in his head, then in longhand. From this manuscript he reads aloud to his wife, whom he calls his "chief editor." Finally the finished version is skillfully typed by his longtime office receptionist.

Of his decision to create, or re-create, the world of the Plains Indian in the 16th and 17th centures, the author says: "There has been very little written about this time period. I wanted also to portray these Native Americans as human beings, rather than as stereotyped 'Indians.' That word does not appear anywhere in the series—for a reason. As I have researched the time and place, the indigenous cultures, it's been a truly inspiring experience for me."

A Proud People In a Harsh Land

THE SPANISH BIT SAGA

Set on the Great Plains of America in the early 16th century, Don Coldsmith's acclaimed series recreates a time, a place and a people that have been nearly lost to history. With the advent of the Spaniards, the horse culture came to the people of the Plains. In THE SPANISH BIT SAGA we see history in the making through the eyes of the proud Native Americans who lived it.

THE SPANISH BIT SAGA
Don Coldsmith

☐ BOOK 1: TRAIL OF THE SPANISH
      BIT   26397 $2.95
☐ BOOK 2: THE ELK-DOG
      HERITAGE   26412 $2.95
☐ BOOK 3: FOLLOW THE WIND   26806 $2.95
☐ BOOK 4: BUFFALO MEDICINE   26938 $2.95
☐ BOOK 5: MAN OF THE SHADOWS   27067 $2.95
☐ BOOK 6: DAUGHTER OF THE
      EAGLE   27209 $2.95
☐ BOOK 7: MOON OF THUNDER   27344 $2.95
☐ BOOK 8: THE SACRED HILLS   27460 $2.95
